*There was no sound* *except for a distant foghorn....*

Did people crash into rocks despite that? Petra wondered. Did they hear the sounds of danger so often they finally lost track of what they meant? Had she been so cautious all her life only to lose it all on a first, desperate throw of the dice?

"Giles . . ." Petra murmured on a thin thread of air, ". . . remember what we talked about."

He raised his head, his eyes dark and slumberous with banked fires. "What was that?"

"Being friends."

He went very still but continued to hold her. Softly, almost sadly, he said, "I'm trying."

"So am I."

"There are times when I even think it's working."

"Me, too."

"And then," he said, "there are times when I wonder why it's important. Men and women have been a lot of things to each other over the ages, but very rarely have they been friends. It hasn't been considered of much value."

"It is to me," she said with quiet firmness.

"It is to me, too," he admitted reluctantly. "The problem is that I don't see being friends with you and desiring you as mutually exclusive."

Dear Reader,

This month brings more excitement your way, starting with Emilie Richards's *The Way Back Home*, the sequel to last month's *Runaway*. Rosie Jensen has taken on another name and begun another life, hoping to be safe from her past. But trouble has a way of catching up to people, and only Grady Clayton—a man who has a lot to lose himself if the truth about Rosie is ever revealed—is strong enough both to love her and to keep her safe.

Paula Detmer Riggs returns us to New Mexico's Santa Ysabel pueblo in *A Lasting Promise*, a book that will bring tears amidst the smiles. Maura Seger is back after too long a time with *Painted Lady*, an intriguing mystery set amongst the beauties of Block Island. And Silhouette Desire favorite Naomi Horton makes her second appearance in the line with *In Safekeeping*.

In months to come look for Linda Howard, Barbara Faith, Emilie Richards (with *Fugitive*, a follow-up to her current duo) and more of your favorites to keep the fires burning here at Silhouette Intimate Moments.

Leslie J. Wainger
Senior Editor and Editorial Coordinator

# Painted Lady

## MAURA SEGER

*Silhouette Intimate Moments*
Published by Silhouette Books New York
**America's Publisher of Contemporary Romance**

SILHOUETTE BOOKS
300 East 42nd St., New York, N.Y. 10017

ISBN: 0-373-07342-9

First Silhouette Books printing July 1990

Printed in the U.S.A.

**Books by Maura Seger**

Silhouette Special Edition

*A Gift Beyond Price* #135

Silhouette Intimate Moments

*Silver Zephyr* #61
*Golden Chimera* #96
*Comes a Stranger* #108
*Shadows of the Heart* #137
*Quest of the Eagle* #149
*Dark of the Moon* #162
*Happily Ever After* #176
*Legacy* #194
*Sea Gate* #209
*Day and Night* #224
*Conflict of Interest* #236
*Unforgettable* #253
*Change of Heart* #280
*Painted Lady* #342

Silhouette Desire

*Cajun Summer* #282
*Treasure Hunt* #295

Silhouette Books

*Silhouette Christmas Stories 1986*
"Starbright"

---

## MAURA SEGER

was prompted by a love of books and a vivid imagination to decide, at age twelve, to be a writer. Twenty years later, her first book was published. So much, she says, for overnight success! Now each book is an adventure, filled with fascinating people who always surprise her.

# Chapter 1

In an instant, the day shattered.

One moment, Giles Chastain was bicycling down a country road. The air was perfumed with honeysuckle, a wood thrush sang in a nearby bush, and off to the side he could see the long stretch of pristine beach where he intended to fish later in the day. He was pleasantly warm, his heartbeat was slow and steady, and he was filled with a sense of well-being.

In the next moment, his body stiffened, his heartbeat accelerated, and he muttered a hard, explicit curse. Around the curve of the road, going too fast and swerving out of control, a moped hurtled straight at him. He hated the demonic little vehicles to start with, had helped lead the unfortunately thwarted campaign to ban them from the island. He didn't need any object lessons to show him how dangerous they were, but it seemed he was about to get one, anyway.

He gripped the handlebars and yanked hard, jerking the bicycle onto the grassy slope beside the road. At first he thought he'd be able to keep his balance, but the ground was bumpier than he'd expected and the impact knocked the bicycle off center. Instinctively he braced himself, let go of the bars and rolled as he fell. He was quickly back on his feet, anger darkening his strong, square-jawed face.

The woman was lying facedown twenty feet away on the other side of the road. She wasn't moving. The moped she'd been riding was on its side next to her.

He crossed the road swiftly and knelt beside her. Her head was obscured by a bright blue helmet. At least she'd had the sense to wear one. Never mind that it was the law, too many moped riders tried to sneak by without one. With luck, she wasn't seriously hurt.

A low moan escaped her. She struggled to sit up.

"Take it easy," Giles said. He was still furiously angry, but simple human compassion outweighed everything else—for the moment. Quickly he ran his hands over her. She was slender, tall for a woman, and undeniably well made. There appeared to be no serious injury that would prevent her from being moved. He slid an arm around her waist to help her turn over, only to stop abruptly when she jerked away from him.

In a muffled voice, she said, "Let go of me."

Giles's dark brown eyes narrowed. He stood up slowly. "Suit yourself." His voice was low and expressionless as he went on, "I'll need your name, address, insurance carrier...the usual. You were exceeding the speed limit and driving on the wrong side of the road. You should turn that thing in—'' he gestured to the moped ''—and try walking instead.''

''Thanks for the tip,'' the woman muttered. She got to her feet, wincing. Giles stood unmoving, watching her. The knuckles of her right hand were cut and bleeding. Her fingers moved stiffly as she undid the strap of her helmet and eased it off.

Red-gold hair, the shade made famous by the painter Titian, tumbled around her shoulders. She raised her head, revealing a heart-shaped face set with startlingly light blue eyes, a delicately formed nose, and a full, lush mouth. It was the kind of face that tended to show up forty feet high on movie screens, or on the covers of glossy magazines. A beautiful, sensual, provocative face.

Giles smiled slightly. It was a cold, assessing smile with more than a hint of cynicism. The face seemed to explain everything—her cavalier disregard for anyone else's safety as well as her misconstruing his efforts to help. With a face like that—and a body to match—a woman wouldn't need to worry about being considerate or fair. She would think, most often correctly, that she would be forgiven anything.

But not this time.

''Your name,'' he said implacably, ''and the rest of it. Unless you'd like to wait until the cops get here?''

She looked startled, then flustered. Her eyes widened, becoming even more impossibly blue and luminous. He wondered if she could do that deliberately.

''No, I don't want to wait,'' she said quietly. ''It was my fault. Just let me find my purse.''

He waited, his patience strained, while she hunted around in the blackberry bushes. She winced again as she bent over and reached into the tangle.

Automatically he took a step forward. "Watch it, they have thorns."

"I should have known," she said ruefully. "They looked so good there had to be a catch."

She straightened up, holding a small, bright red clutch purse. It clashed aggressively with her hair, not to mention with the orange pedal pushers that hugged her slim hips. With them, she wore a purple shirt festooned with small green stars.

Giles smiled again, this time more genuinely. Only a truly beautiful woman could get away with such an outfit. Whatever else she was, she was certainly no fashion plate.

"That's . . . uh . . . quite a getup."

Head down, rifling through her purse, she murmured, "It's an original Xanadu. *Vogue* called it 'scintillating,' and *WWD* said it signaled a return to 'gay, rambunctious clothing.' I gather you don't agree."

Giles shook his head slightly, as though trying to clear it. "What's *WWD*?"

It was her turn to look perplexed. "*Women's Wear Daily*, the bible of the fashion industry. I thought everyone knew that."

"Apparently not. I apologize for my ignorance. Now, if you wouldn't mind . . ."

"Here it is." She withdrew the relevant information with a flourish that suggested she was pleasantly surprised to have found it. As she handed the insurance card to Giles, she said softly, "Look, I'm sorry if I seemed a little defensive a few minutes ago. I'd gotten the wind knocked out of me and wasn't sure what was going on."

"That's fine." Without looking at her, he withdrew a small black case from his pocket. Inside was a pad of paper and a gold fountain pen.

He glanced down at the card. Petra O'Toole. Address on the west side of Manhattan. The birth date made her twenty-six.

"I'll get the bike checked out this afternoon. If there's much damage, you'll be notified. Otherwise, we'll forget it."

Her mouth twitched. "That's fine."

It took him a moment to realize that she was mimicking him. He smiled again, slowly, the smile Amanda had called "inscrutable." He wondered what *WWD* would have made of it.

"My name is Giles Chastain, by the way, and I meant what I said about getting rid of that thing. It would be a shame to have your visit spoiled any further."

Petra hesitated. She was struck by a sudden, outrageous impulse to suggest how he could not only make her visit unspoiled, but a resounding success. A personal tour of the island, or dinner, perhaps. After all, it wasn't every day that a woman ran into six feet plus, two hundred muscled pounds of tawny blond male. And that look he had—something to do with the eyes and the mouth—that very strong hint that this was an actual, dyed-in-the-wool *man*, not a boy masquerading as such.

Not that it mattered. She could as soon give him the slightest encouragement as she could flap her wings and fly to the moon. The mere fact that she even thought of it amazed her. The fall must have affected her more than she'd realized.

"I'm not as dumb as I may look, Mr. Chastain," she said softly. "My mopeding days are over as soon as I get back to the lot. If you're through with that." She held out her hand for the card.

He returned it slowly. For a moment they stared at each other—the tall, golden-haired man with the hard, weathered face and the slender, vibrant young woman with the faint sense of sadness hanging about her.

Reluctantly they remembered themselves.

"Thanks," Petra murmured as she got back up on the moped.

Giles nodded, feeling curiously reluctant to see her go. That was foolish. She was far too young and too...vivacious?...vital? No, that wasn't right. It made him sound like an old fogy, which he certainly wasn't.

He was merely a quiet and studious man, a historian by profession, who preferred the more genteel past to the strident and hectic present. Of which this young lady was very much a part, at least if the "gay, rambunctious clothing" was any indication. The figure, however, was eternal—high, firm breasts, slim waist, slender hips and legs that never seemed to end. Enough to make even an old fogy forget his best resolve.

A dull flush crept over her cheeks. He realized suddenly that his thoughts were only too evident, but he was startled by her reaction. She looked away hastily and switched on the moped, almost as though she were afraid.

"Thanks again," she murmured. In a moment she was gone down the road and out of sight.

An hour later, Giles returned home. He parked the bicycle beside the old oak tree that held pride of place on the front lawn. Ahead of him was the house his great-aunt Emmeline had willed to him. The house that never failed to provoke a startled stare and a wistful smile from all who saw it.

It was a folly, a white elephant, a great and glorious extravaganza of Victoriana in all its gingerbread finery. Giles loved it with the half-abashed but unapologetic love of a man who has found something for which he's always hankered. It was his version of an extravagant sailboat or an expensive sports car. Not coincidentally, just as either of those would have, the house absorbed a great deal of his time and income.

He carried his bag of groceries into the kitchen, unpacked it and put the contents away in the restaurant-size refrigerator. Directly across from it was a professional gas stove complete with six burners and adjacent broiler. The cabinets were pickled pine, the floor, red oak covered by an Ezine, made fifty-odd years ago on the plains of Anatolia close to the ruins of Troy. The rug was one of two dozen such Orientals scattered around the house, also courtesy of Great-aunt Emmeline. But the kitchen itself was new, installed the year before. Giles had sunk much of the royalties from one of his books into the renovation. He hadn't regretted it for a moment.

He glanced at the large railroad clock on the wall as he headed upstairs. Ten minutes later he was in the backyard. Stripped to the waist, wearing only black sweatpants, he went through a half hour of rigorous exercise beginning with a series of rhythmic t'ai chi ch'uan movements and ending with a karate workout. When he was done, his powerful chest glistened, the ribbed muscles gleaming as though oiled. He was breathing hard but felt pleasantly tired.

Upstairs, he soaked in the claw-footed tub before dressing in a fresh pair of khaki pants and a plain white shirt. He was on his way out of the house when the phone rang. For a moment, he considered letting it go, but his conscience pricked him. As soon as he heard the voice on the other end he regretted not following his impulse. Paul Delacroix was an old friend and a former colleague, but he could also be a royal pain in the butt.

"No, I haven't changed my mind," Giles said with quiet firmness. "State can get on fine without me."

An exasperated snort filtered down the secure line from Washington. "You know this thing with China could go up in flames."

"You're exaggerating. It's all very unfortunate, but we've been through worse before. The lower the profile we keep now, the better."

"We may not have that choice. They're talking about starting up the executions again. Friends of yours are on the lists."

Giles's eyes were bleak. At that instant, he hated Paul for so forcibly reminding him of what he was still trying desperately to forget.

"They're bluffing. They know if there are any more killings, the World Bank will turn off the money tap. With the Chinese economy going down the tubes, they can't let that happen."

"Maybe, and maybe they don't give a flying you-know-what. They're old men, Giles. They're going to die soon, and they aren't so anxious to go alone."

"They won't be," Giles said quietly. "They killed two thousand in Tiananmen Square and at least another ten thousand elsewhere. Compared to the massacres of the past, it may not seem like much, but they'll be remembered forever."

"You can still help," Paul began.

"Only if I stay away. I'd be recognized immediately, and anyone I came into contact with would be in danger."

"We're not asking you to go back in," Paul protested. "Hell, we were lucky to get you out the last time, we don't want to go through that again. But we do want the benefit of your insight. You were born in Hong Kong and you lived in China for years. You know the lay of the land better than just about anyone."

"That's a crock, Paul, and we both know it. I was never anything but an amateur. You've got plenty of China pros. Try listening to them for a change."

"They all talk the same diplomatic garbage," the assistant secretary of state complained. "'On the one hand, this, on the other hand, that.' You were always a hell of a lot more direct.''

Despite himself, Giles laughed. ''Only because we always talked over a couple of beers after we'd worn ourselves out playing handball. *And* I didn't have a career riding on whatever I said.''

''You missed your calling,'' Paul complained. ''You should have been at State or maybe even with the Company, instead of trying to teach history to a bunch of snot-nosed college kids.''

''Some of those kids have plenty going for them,'' Giles countered. ''Besides, I *like* British history and I like teaching, both a hell of a lot more than I like State, forget the CIA. Look, you want my opinion on China, I'll be happy to give it to you. But I'm not coming back to Washington. The climate's lousy and the fishing stinks.''

Paul chuckled. ''Yeah, but the women aren't half bad. I ran into Amanda at an embassy party the other night. That's one very foxy lady who still seems hung up on you.''

Giles's eyes hardened. ''Not a chance. She's trawling for much bigger game, someone who's as turned on by power as she is. Watch you don't get your fingers burned.''

Paul pretended to be shocked. ''Buddy boy, would I do a thing like that? Amanda was strictly private stock. Far as I'm concerned, she still is.''

''Stow it, friend. You want some free advice or don't you?''

The assistant secretary sighed. ''Talk, pal, I'm listening.''

An hour later, after taking the other man step-by-step through his analysis of the current China situation, Giles finally got off the phone. He glanced at his watch ruefully. So much for a peaceful day on bucolic Block Island. His fishing time was shot, and he still had page proofs to read.

At least he could take them out to the porch swing. He settled there, under a spreading oak tree, and turned dutifully to the tiresome but necessary task. Inevitably his attention wandered, but not in any direction he could have expected.

Instead of replaying his conversation with Delacroix or, worse yet, drifting to thoughts of Amanda, he found himself thinking about Titian hair and crystalline blue eyes. He almost regretted that the bike had only the most minor damage. There was no reason for him to have any further contact with Petra O'Toole.

No reason at all.

Petra turned over on her stomach and glanced surreptitiously at her watch. At once she felt foolish. She was completely alone; there was no one to observe her impatience.

She was supposed to be having fun. Wasn't that what most people thought of lying in the sun on a beautiful stretch of beach with nothing to do and nowhere to go? Fun. *Hah*. She was bored out of her skull. Her skin itched, the suntan lotion she'd put on smelled funny, and the bestseller she'd brought along to read sounded exactly like ten other books she'd read in the past year. Face it, she wasn't a beach person.

But what else was there to do? She'd tried walking, only to discover that the shoes that were fine for running around the block to the deli in didn't feel so great after the first mile or so. She had the blisters to prove it.

She'd checked out the shops but figured she could live without a plastic coffee cup emblazoned with a lobster, or a T-shirt that said, "Frankly scallop, I don't give a clam."

She could try blackberry-picking if she didn't mind getting her skin torn off, but she wasn't sure what she'd do with the things once she had them.

And she was saving the library for when she got really desperate.

Three weeks to go. She stifled a groan. Daphne had meant well. When her agent had offered her the house on Block Island, Petra's first instinct had been to refuse.

Before she could, Daphne had put her hands on her hips, narrowed her eyes and said, "You look awful, you aren't eating or sleeping, and the less said about your work, the better. When normal people get like that, they know they need a rest. Now, do you want to go voluntarily or do you have to be hog-tied and carried?"

She went. The first few days weren't bad. She had only the usual minor vertigo that Manhattan cavern dwellers get when confronted by too much uninterrupted sky. The quiet was a little unsettling, but she could live with it. The only problem was figuring out what to do with herself. Hence, the moped. Hence, Giles Chastain. Hence...hence...hence... Oh, the hell with it. She wasn't going to be able to relax and that was that. There was only one thing to do in such a situation.

Work. Long, hard, blessed work. Never mind that it was cheating to work while on vacation. She'd just have to live with that extra little bit of guilt.

Immensely cheered, she rose, rolled up the blanket and left the beach.

An hour later, she was on her knees fiddling with the focus on one of the three cameras hanging around her neck. It felt great to be back in the groove. As long as she kept busy enough, there was no reason why she shouldn't breeze through the rest of her stay.

No reason at all.

## Chapter 2

Two days later, one week after her arrival on the island, Petra gazed longingly at the departing ferry. She had seriously considered taking it. Only her refusal to cravenly accept defeat stopped her. She was going to stick this out no matter what.

Glumly she stirred her coffee and tried to concentrate on the newspaper. The hotel porch was crowded. All around her couples were chatting, parents were soothing their children, life was going on.

She seemed to be the only person there who was alone. Maybe that was part of the problem, although she'd never minded her own company before. On the contrary, she'd always felt most comfortable by herself. Until now. On this tiny island, miles from the mainland, where solitude was supposed to be a way of life, she was having her first close encounter with loneliness.

"Will there be anything else, miss?"

Jolted from her thoughts, Petra looked up at the waiter. "No, thanks, just the check."

She paid and left, walking determinedly down the street. So her work was suddenly no longer the cure-all it had always been. She was still going to keep busy. The kitchen in Daphne's house looked as though it had never been used—not surprising, considering her agent's conviction that a meal not eaten out was a meal wasted. Petra herself had never cooked much, but she knew one end of a spatula from the other. She might as well give it a try.

The fish store was quiet and pleasantly dark after the brilliant sunshine outside. One wall was taken up by stainless steel lobster tanks. A glass counter ran down the center displaying an assortment of seafood laid out on beds of ice. For the first time in a while, she felt hungry.

Or she did until the door swung open again and she caught a glimpse of the man who had just entered. Instinctively she stiffened.

He had stopped right inside the door and was looking at her. They eyed each other for several long moments before Giles cleared his throat.

"Miss O'Toole, nice to see you again."

His voice sounded husky. Petra wondered if he was coming down with a cold. Nasty things, summer colds. It would be a shame if he caught one. Those glorious amber-brown eyes would turn red, that long, firm nose would drip, that mouth would...

"Mr. Chastain," she croaked, "how nice."

Giles stared at her. He'd more or less convinced himself that her hair couldn't possibly be the exact shade of glittering red-gold that he remembered, but it was. Her eyes were as enthralling, her lips as soft and full, her skin as creamy.

"Nice," he echoed.

They stood, staring at each other, until the boy behind the counter interrupted them. He gave them a look of bemusement combined with derision, as though people their age should have more sense than to act like that in public. It was okay for people *his* age, but definitely unseemly for anyone else.

"What'll you have?" he demanded.

"Uh...I'm not sure," Petra said. "Why don't you go ahead?" she suggested to Giles.

He had completely ignored the boy and was still looking at her. His eyes crinkled slightly as he smiled. "That's okay. I'm not in any hurry."

"I can come back," the boy muttered sarcastically.

"Fine," Giles said. "Why don't you do that?"

The boy's mouth opened, shut, opened again. He was beginning to resemble one of the fish on the ice in front of him. The shattering of his illusions about people over twenty, and the sudden possibilities that opened up for his future self, had him stymied.

"Yes," Petra added helpfully, "why don't you?"

She looked at Giles again and laughed. At that instant, she felt younger than the boy. As though twenty-six difficult years counted for nothing. The sensation was disconcerting, bewildering, and very welcome.

"How have you been?" Giles asked softly. He stood with his hands thrust deep into his pockets, his long legs planted slightly apart. His hair was rumpled, and he hadn't shaved yet that day. He might have just gotten out of bed.

Petra's throat tightened as she contemplated the images that conjured up, and she murmured, "Fine, thanks. How about yourself? And the bike, too, of course?"

"The bike's fine and so am I." He reached out suddenly, his bronzed hand emerging from his pants pocket. His touch was warm and gentle as he lifted the fingers she had scraped.

"You're sure, no ill effects?"

Her eyes glittered until she quickly blinked. She was unaccustomed to such concern, even if it was motivated only by courtesy.

"None at all," she said, pushing aside the uneasy boredom, the stirring memory, the presence of this man who had been on the edge of her thoughts since their first, brief meeting.

He nodded and let go of her hand. Oddly bereft, she drew it behind her back.

"Are you enjoying yourself?" he asked.

Petra hesitated. She had never acquired the necessary skills for lying and was reluctant to display her clumsiness. Candidly she said, "It's a bit of an adjustment from New York."

Giles laughed softly. "I'll bet. Are you here on your own?"

A tiny flutter, like the wings of a bird, moved under her breasts. Beneath it, restless and dark, loomed the cavern of her own ineptitude.

She looked away, focusing on the dead fish in the case. "Yes, I am."

Giles was surprised. He had half expected her to mention a boyfriend or husband. She wore no wedding or engagement ring, but that wasn't always a certain indicator these days. More telling was the fact that any man with an ounce of sense wouldn't have let her go wandering around by herself so much. Men had changed much less in that regard than many women seemed to think. They still clung to a certain possessive protectiveness as a way of warning off potential interlopers.

"So am I," Giles said.

Petra was momentarily confused. "What? Oh, alone...I see, well...are you enjoying yourself?"

"Yes, I am. I like it here. But then I'm much more familiar with the place than I suppose you are. It takes time to feel at home."

Petra laughed faintly. "In my case, it would probably take a personality transplant. I'm a city person."

Giles hesitated. What exactly was she telling him? He was attracted to her and was reasonably sure that she felt the same way about him. But in the hasty scramble of the modern mating dance, there were those who preferred not to waste time or effort. They tried to establish compatibility within the first few minutes, instantly rejecting those who didn't seem to fit whatever they were looking for—be it a one-night stand or a lifetime commitment.

Yet Petra didn't give the impression of being either so desperate or so impetuous. There was something closed-off and quiet about her that he found tantalizing.

He smiled inwardly. Without being vain, he knew that women had always made it easy for him. It was predictable that he'd finally be drawn to one who didn't.

"Since we're both on our own," Giles said, "would you care to join me for dinner?"

Petra had anticipated the question; she was hardly so naive that she didn't realize where they were headed. What did elude her was how to respond. She'd always held back from relationships, doubting her ability to do more than make a hash of them. Her recent experience with Daryl only seemed to confirm that.

Yet she was drawn to Giles Chastain. She liked his steadiness, the intelligence she felt in him, the quiet sense of competency he projected. She was also acutely aware of him on another, more basic level.

And when all was said and done, what harm could there be in a single dinner?

"I'd like that," she said softly.

His eyes crinkled at the corners. "Good. I'll give you directions to my place." Quickly he added, "That is, if you don't mind. The restaurants tend to be very crowded at this time of year, and I'm a pretty fair cook."

Relieved not so much by his explanation as by the fact that he'd had the sensitivity to offer it, Petra nodded. "That's fine. I was planning to cook tonight myself. How about if we join forces? I'll bring the appetizer."

The boy sidled over but kept a cautious eye on Giles. "Ready now, sir?"

"The lady is first."

Petra gave her order, trying not to show her amusement. The byplay between the boy and Giles was subtle but entertaining. It wasn't all that different from the male dominance rituals she'd observed while photographing primates in New Guinea. But she doubted any female primate had ever felt the burgeoning sense of anticipation that tightened her stomach and sent a wave of warmth washing through her. She was looking forward to dinner with Giles more than was probably wise.

She left him a short time later, the directions to his house in her bag. They looked simple enough. He said he lived on the beach at the end of an unpaved road. She envisioned a simple cottage in keeping with the man's apparently straightforward and unpretentious tastes.

She was wrong.

Petra stepped out of her car slowly. She thought she was in the right place, yet she didn't know how she could be. The house rising before her looked like something out of a dream. Moreover, there was nothing remotely straightforward or unpretentious about it.

Bemusedly she took in the sweep of the high, dormered roof enhanced at one corner by a turret complete with filigreed widow's walk. Beneath, running the full width of the house and disappearing around both corners, was a deep, shaded porch. Twin brick chimneys rose against the sky. An immense oak tree dominated the full lawn, but behind it Petra could make out a series of trellises heavy with honeysuckle and roses.

Beautiful, exquisite, enthralling...also pink. Well, to be fair, not exactly pink. The house was done in varying shades of mauve and rose, the roof and trim in blue-gray and white. The combination was perfect if startling.

"Oh, Lord," she murmured under her breath. No simple man lived in such a house. He had to be a good deal more complicated than she'd thought.

He was also coming down the porch steps to greet her.

"Hi," Giles said quietly. His eyes swept over her. She looked startled and apprehensive. Instinctively he sought to soothe her. "Is anything wrong?"

"Wrong? Oh, no, nothing." She conjured up a smile. "Everything's fine. What an...incredible house."

So that was it. The house had knocked her off balance. He'd felt the same way the first time he had seen it. "Really something, isn't she?" he asked.

Petra's eyebrows rose. "She?"

He shrugged unapologetically. "'It' doesn't seem right, and 'he' sure doesn't fit. Besides, the house was built for a woman, my great-aunt Emmeline. She put a lot of her own personality into it.''

Petra took another long look at the results. "She must have been a remarkable woman."

"She was a holy terror," Giles said good-naturedly. "At least that's how I remember her. I only met her a few times when I was a kid. It was quite a surprise when she left me the place."

"Do you live here full-time?" Petra asked as they mounted the steps to the porch.

"I'm not sure," Giles said. He opened the front door and stood aside for her to precede him. "This is my first year here. I haven't decided yet whether or not I'll stay through the winter, although there's no reason why I couldn't."

So there was nothing pressing to take him from the island. Unusual man to have so few demands on his time and attention.

"It must be nice," she said, "not to have to go racing back to a job."

"I write," he explained as they entered the front hall. "I also used to teach history at Georgetown University in Washington, but I'm on a leave of absence." He didn't add that he had the option to make that leave permanent. He was still undecided about returning to teaching, but if he did, there were a number of other positions available to him.

The entry hall was wide and cool. Paneled mahogany walls glowed faintly. Petra caught the scent of fresh flowers on an inlaid table. Twelve feet above her, the ceiling was festooned with grinning cherubs.

The deeply rooted practical side of her nature would not be constrained. She said what almost any woman seeing the house for the first time would think. "You don't take care of this place yourself?"

"Not exactly," Giles said with a laugh. "A neighbor comes in to clean. My contribution has been mainly time and money. Houses like this tend to soak up both."

"I can imagine," Petra murmured. She thought of her own apartment in the SoHo section of downtown Manhattan. If she hadn't been as successful at her work as she was, she never would have been able to afford the renovations needed to make it livable. But this . . .

They went on into the kitchen. She handed him the plastic container she'd brought with their appetizer. She'd considered cooking the scallops, but she really preferred them raw, as seviche, and had decided to take a chance that he wouldn't mind too much. Glancing around at the restaurant-sized appliances, she said, "I guess this doesn't really count as cooking."

He glanced inside the container and his face brightened. "Seviche, one of my favorites. Sure it counts. Would you like a glass of wine while I get the rest ready?"

She nodded and perched on a high wooden stool next to the counter, where he had laid out various implements. The wine was dry and crisp. The glass he served it in was fluted crystal.

The kitchen was immaculate—from the copper pots hanging on wrought-iron hooks to the magnificent

Oriental rug underfoot. Giles himself looked cool and competent in pleated khaki trousers and a light blue shirt crossed by dark red suspenders. The clothes were almost but not quite preppy—expensive, comfortable with a touch of whimsy. They suited him.

He was busy taking items from the enormous refrigerator. Clearly he hadn't been boasting when he said he knew how to cook. He was comfortably at home in the kitchen of this rose-hued house.

Petra frowned slightly. He lived alone, no female companion in sight. He wrote and had been a teacher. He spoke gently when he wasn't angry, and she felt instinctively reassured in his presence despite her usual nervousness around men. He liked to cook, he cherished an old and intensely romantic house.

Was it possible, she wondered, that her hormones were firing in the wrong direction?

She looked down at her glass. There was no way to ask, and besides, did it really matter? The best she'd ever managed with a man was friendship. Maybe when it came right down to it, that was the best there was.

Petra raised her head and smiled. "May I help?"

"Sure." He put her to work on the salad as he deftly cracked the shell of the lobster he had already cooked. He removed the meat and placed it in a large pan with butter, garlic and a touch of dry vermouth. Petra's nose twitched appreciatively.

Giles turned his attention to a machine next to him that looked like a cross between a food processor and a dough mixer. He measured flour and water into it, added a handful of spinach and a couple eggs, and flicked the machine on. Moments later, perfect strands of spinach pasta emerged from one end. These he lowered in a wire-mesh basket into boiling water, shaking them lightly for a minute or two as they cooked, then quickly removing them.

He flashed her a grin. "We eat."

The dining room was softly lit. Shadows drifted in the corners of the plum-toned walls, beneath the ceiling crested with ornate plaster moldings. A bronze-and-silver chandelier threw a circle of light over the table covered in white lace and set with fresh flowers.

"Beautiful," Petra murmured.

"Appropriate," Giles said. "I don't mind ripping out the kitchen, but I've tried to keep the rest pretty much as it was."

"I'm sure Emmeline would be grateful for that."

He laughed. "I doubt she was ever grateful for a thing in her life. It wasn't her style. If she were here now, she'd probably tell me to gut the place and turn it into condominiums."

"If she felt that way," Petra asked, "why did she leave it to you?"

"Because I was the only family she had," he explained quietly. "She'd outlived everyone else."

Slowly Petra digested this. "Then you're an only child. So am I."

He nodded, as though that confirmed what he had already guessed. "Are you close to your family?"

Petra shook her head. "How about you?"

Giles hesitated. He didn't usually go into details about his family, but he sensed that if he was to learn more about Petra, he would have to open up about himself first. He didn't care to examine too closely why he was willing to do that.

Slowly he said, "My father was killed in Hong Kong where he was serving with the British consul. I was eight years old at the time. My mother and I went to live with her family in the States. She remarried a short time later, and a few years after that she died."

Petra was silent for several moments. At length, she said, "I suppose I should ask you about Hong Kong first. That's less personal and therefore more polite. But I'm really interested in what happened to your mother. She couldn't have been very old when she died."

Giles put his fork down. Outside, beyond the windows draped in lacy white curtains, twilight lay gently over the rolling lawns and old stone walls that screened the house from the beach. A cool breeze ruffled the trees. At the most distant limit of his vision, along the shadowed line where earth, water and sky all met, he could see the flickering lights of the mainland.

"She was thirty-five, three years older than I am now. I remember her as very beautiful and full of life, although I didn't really see that much of her. She had come from a great deal of money and was used to doing pretty much anything she pleased, but none of it seemed to make her very happy. With hindsight, I realize that her behavior became increasingly destructive after my father's death. She never seemed to get over him despite having remarried. Finally one night she took one too many sleeping pills washed down by one too many shots of whiskey. She just never woke up."

Petra let her breath out slowly. Platitudes were not her strong suit; besides, she despised them. She said what was in her heart.

"I'm sorry for her, but she had no right to leave a young boy on his own the way she did."

Giles shrugged. "I didn't have any claim on her."

"You were her child. There is no greater claim."

He looked at her curiously. Few women of his acquaintance spoke so clearly of their feelings about children. Indeed, few spoke of them at all. Amanda, for instance, had been reticent on that subject alone. On all others she had been persistently voluble.

"What about you?" he asked. "You don't see much of your parents?"

Petra looked back down at her plate. Thick russet lashes shielded her eyes. She'd brought the subject up; she owed him a reply. It was best to get it over with as quickly as possible. "They divorced when I was five. I moved back and forth between the two of them until I was eighteen. After that, I guess we'd all had enough of one another. We still stay in touch, but that's about it."

Giles supected that the bare recital concealed a far vaster well of emotion, but he was disinclined to probe it. All else aside, he had no right to.

"The seviche is excellent, by the way," he said gently.

Her eyes brightened. They were almost the same shade as the soft silk dress she wore. It lay in graceful folds over her high breasts and slim waist, fitting smoothly around her hips to fall in a wide arc to the middle of her calves. The dress had a pleasingly old-

fashioned look to it, almost as though she had anticipated the house. Then he remembered reading something about a new trend toward highly feminine and
romantic clothes, and hid a smile. Miss O'Toole was
thoroughly modern even when she was skirting the
past.

She had left her hair down. In the fading light, it
looked shot through with bolts of gold.

They talked of other things. Petra told him a little
about being a photographer, but there was much she
didn't say. She didn't mention the several books published, the gallery shows, the frequent magazine
spreads. To her, none of that mattered a great deal.
What counted were the photographs themselves.

"Have you done much since you got here?" he
asked.

She shook her head. "I don't really know what the
problem is, but it's definitely there. Every time I try to
get back to work, I run up against some kind of wall."

"This place is probably too pretty."

Petra stared at him. She was always impressed by
someone who could hit the nail on the head like that,
especially with just a handful of words.

"It's true," she said, "I don't take pretty pictures."

"It didn't sound like you did. I'll tell you what, how
about if I take you someplace tomorrow where I think
you'll find plenty worth photographing?"

A spurt of excitement darted through her, inspired
only partly by the possibility of finally doing some
decent work. There was also the fact that she would be
with Giles.

"Some place on the island?" she asked.

"No, every place here is flat-out gorgeous. Even the garbage dump is picturesque. But I've got a boat, and if you're willing to trust me, I don't think you'll be disappointed."

Petra hesitated only a second before she nodded.

## Chapter 3

Petra woke before dawn. She lay on her back, looking up at the ceiling, and listened to the stirrings of the birds just beyond the windows.

How quiet it was. She could hear only the birds and the wind. That and her own heartbeat.

She had slept little, yet she felt well rested. It was after midnight when she had left Giles. They had lingered long on the curved porch, looking out over the darkened sea, sipping wine and talking. He had lived in New York for a while and knew many of the places she frequented, though it was clear he hadn't found them very entertaining. He was too polite to say so straight out, but she gathered that the ceaseless to and fro of New York social life had bored him.

She stretched, feeling her body move beneath her thin cotton nightgown, and the sheet and blanket she had needed the night before. Already the air was warming. It would be a hot day.

She showered and dressed before busying herself with her cameras. Still not knowing where they were going, except that it was by boat, she prepared as best she could. Just as she had finished, Giles arrived.

He stood in the door, his head tilted slightly to one side, looking at her. A faint smile played over his mouth. He'd awakened to thoughts of the previous evening and to the conviction that it couldn't have been quite as he remembered. They had been too comfortable with each other after the initial awkwardness. He'd felt completely relaxed with Petra in a way that puzzled him when he thought back to it. Normally he was far more guarded. Now, seeing her in the morning light, he felt again the tantalizing puzzle of having been with someone he felt he had known for a very long time, yet had only just met.

"Ready?" he murmured, his eyes sweeping her. She looked very fresh and young in bright green shorts and an equally bright yellow T-shirt. A purple sweater lay next to her camera bag. She had on pink sneakers tied with purple laces. Her hair was braided and coiled at the back of her head. She had tied a purple ribbon through it.

He touched it lightly with his finger. "You like this color."

"I like all colors," she said. She breathed in the nearness of him, the crisp, sun-warmed scent, the heady male strength. Then she remembered the gentle pink house, the white lace, and again felt confusion.

"And yet," Giles said, "you seem to work mainly in black-and-white." His attention had been caught by the photographs lying on the table. There were several dozen of them. Some he could see completely, others offered only a corner or two. All were of people caught in a hundred poses, mainly brittle and self-conscious, some bordering on sad.

"What are these?" he asked.

Petra was flustered. She had forgotten about leaving the photos out when she left to have dinner the night before, and by the time she'd gotten home, she'd been too tired to put them away. Now they stared up at Giles in all their revealing intensity.

"I took them in New York," she said as she quickly began to scoop them away. "I've just been printing them here."

"You have a darkroom?"

She nodded. "The house belongs to my agent. She does some photography herself and installed the darkroom as a convenience."

It flitted through Giles's mind that her agent must be fairly successful to afford the small but well-situated cottage complete with such luxuries as a darkroom. The previous evening, listening to Petra talk about her work, he'd gotten the impression that she was very successful without her saying so. Now he was more certain than ever. It would explain much about her, particularly her self-sufficiency. She didn't need someone else to give her life shape and meaning.

Which made her all the more compelling to a man wary of being used.

He didn't mention the photos again, respectful of her obvious unwillingness to discuss them. But he promised himself that he would see them again soon, and through them, see more of the spirit of this beautiful but oddly vulnerable young woman.

He had come for her in an old, battered Land Rover, the kind that looked as though it would be more at home on the plains of Kenya or forging mountain streams near Kathmandu. It took the paved roads grudgingly.

Few people were about. They reached the boat basin quickly. Petra followed Giles to the edge of the water where a rubber dinghy bobbed.

"Hold tight," he advised with a smile as he got the motor going and steered them away from shore. The harbor lay between dune-draped headlands, reachable only by a narrow cleft that was the door to the sea. Beyond the wharfs, a hundred or more boats rode at anchor. Most were small cabin cruisers, a few qualified as yachts. But it was the sailboats that intrigued Petra. She had always been fascinated by the notion that sails could capture wind and use it to conquer distance.

Ahead, glimmering in the sun, lay a particularly magnificent double-masted schooner. It looked like something out of another age, as though it had sailed into the harbor through the mists of time itself. Yet it was vividly, excitingly, real.

She was delighted but not overly surprised when Giles brought the dinghy up next to it. He went aboard first, then helped her up, apologizing for the primitive rope ladder.

"I haven't had too many visitors," he said. "*Popo* was in pretty bad shape when I got her. It's taken a while to get her to the point where she's presentable."

Petra's eyebrows rose. "*Popo*? That seems like a frivolous name for such a majestic boat."

Giles smiled. "She is something, isn't she? Her full name is *Feng-p'o-p'o*; she was named for the Chinese goddess of the wind, who is said to ride a tiger among the clouds."

"Oh." Not frivolous at all and another insight into this complicated man. His father's death in Hong Kong had not broken Giles's attachment to the East. He seemed to still carry that with him.

"Have you spent much time in China?" she asked. "I mean, since you were a child."

He showed her into the wheelhouse before he replied. "I lived on the mainland for three years, mostly in Beijing."

"When did you leave?"

His back was to her. She couldn't see his face as he said, "In the summer, after the demonstrations."

Summer? Surely he meant the spring; the blood-drenched spring of shattered hopes and brutal death when China had exploded in savage repression.

"You stayed . . . ?" she murmured.

"There were things to do."

He did not elaborate. She did not ask. But unspoken between them was the knowledge that the "things" he had done had been neither easy nor safe. His spirit remained scarred by them.

She waited until he had raised the anchor chains and hoisted the first jib sail. They were moving slowly out of the harbor when she said, "Once when I was a little girl, I saw a terrible automobile accident. It happened almost in front of the house where my father was living. Five people were injured. I remember standing on the sidewalk crying. My father thought I was frightened, but I was actually furious. I knew that I couldn't make a difference in any way, and I hated feeling so helpless. It made me angry at everything and everyone."

Giles looked at her for what seemed like a long time before he said softly, "I'm not angry, at least not anymore. I'm just...tired."

She took a step toward him and held out her hand. "Then sit down and rest. I happen to be a pretty fair sailor."

She wasn't exaggerating. As he watched her, he thought that she looked perfectly at home with her hands braced lightly on either side of the wheel. *Feng-p'o-p'o* must have agreed, for the schooner responded to her slightest touch. Giles smiled and sat back against the deep cushions that covered the bench.

Petra cast him a quick look. Even with the wheel in her hands, she couldn't quite believe that he had surrendered the boat to her. When she'd suggested it, she'd been only half serious. Not that she was sorry. The feel of the magnificent schooner was unlike any other she had known. But even in the midst of enjoying the experience, she was mindful that very few men would have permitted it. Or if they had, they would have hovered nearby, instructing and adjusting until swiftly reclaiming their prerogative.

Giles wasn't like that. He seemed perfectly content to sit back and let her take charge. Did he know that freedom like that constituted a highly elastic bond? The further it was allowed to stretch the more forcefully it bounced back.

"Where are we heading?" she asked.

"North by northwest." He gave her the coordinates then watched silently as she made the necessary adjustments. When they were on course, he said, "You're good. Where did you learn to sail?"

"I went to camp in the summer, and on winter breaks I was usually sent off to learn something or other. I didn't take to most of it, but I learned to love sailing."

"It shows," he said, thinking of the child she had been. He wasn't so naive as to believe her experience was unusual; literally millions of children have had to cope with divorce. But the numbers didn't make it any easier to bear. His situation had been more dramatic yet also somehow more clear-cut.

Several minutes later, Petra cleared her throat. Discreetly she asked, "Do you think you could tell me now what we'll be seeing?"

"Boats," Giles said succinctly. "Lots of boats."

She felt a twinge of disappointment. Sailing aside, she didn't have much use for boats. She'd long ago taken all the photos of them that she could ever imagine wanting. A print of *Feng-p'o-p'o* might be nice to have as a remembrance, but apart from that, she felt no enthusiasm for the idea.

Giles watched the play of emotion across her face and smiled gently. "Don't worry. They aren't pretty."

She cast him a quizzical look. "They aren't?"

"Nope. Neither are the people on them. But they are real."

Half an hour later, she saw what he meant. They came into the harbor at Point Judith and swung around to dock near a busy wharf. Giles took the controls then as Petra quickly brought down the sails. She didn't feel up to squeezing the schooner into the tiny available spot. At the very least, she'd scratch the paint.

They left the boat riding securely at anchor and crossed the wharf. On the other side, amid a tangle of ropes, crates and chains, several men were clustered around a trawler. The boat was battered and stained, the paint peeling and rust evident on the anchor winch. But the deck itself was clean, and the equipment stacked on board was neat and ordered.

"I thought fishing boats went out before dawn," Petra said.

"They used to, but it's getting tougher these days to bring in a decent catch. Also tougher to muster a crew. When I called Dave last night, he said he thought he'd be making a second run about now."

Dave turned out to be a young man, in his thirties, with sandy hair, weathered skin and weary eyes. He clasped hands with Giles and nodded shyly to Petra.

"Nice to meet you, miss. Any friend of Giles's is always welcome on the *Windstar*."

"Thanks," she said softly. "I hope I won't be in the way."

Dave assured her she wouldn't be. He talked briefly with Giles about where they would be going, while

Petra listened and looked around. Automatically she readied one camera and took a few quick shots. Moments later, they cast off.

She found a place for herself sitting on a closed hatchway while Giles went to help the crew. He worked easily with them, as though he had done it many times before. They moved smoothly out into the sound. As the sun rose higher and the day warmed, Petra removed her sweater. She wished she could have taken off more, but that was hardly possible. Giles and the other men felt no such constraint. They stripped to the waist.

All were young and fit, but none had the tensile strength, the perfectly sculpted muscles, the long, graceful sinews of Giles. Try though she did, Petra couldn't keep from looking at him. His upper body was as bronzed as his face. Soft, curling hairs gleamed across his chest and tapered in a darkening line to vanish below his waist. As he moved, hauling on the ropes, she could see the powerful muscles of his thighs and calves straining and releasing.

She swallowed nervously and gripped her camera. Determinedly, she left her perch and began to move cautiously along the deck. Whereas *Feng-p'o-p'o* had moved through the swells with easy grace, *Windstar* made no such attempt. Despite her romantic name, she was a strong, lumbering vessel that got along more through brute strength and determination than ability.

The camera lens was always her most trustworthy eye. Through it she could capture the dark, hard sweep of the deck, the tense bunches of men, their strained faces, the anxious but proud look of the captain himself as Dave maneuvered through the fishing beds.

It was hard, dirty work in the heat of the sun with barely a breeze for relief. Again and again, the nets were lowered, trawled and recovered. Even half empty as they returned, they weighed hundreds of pounds. Backs strained, muscles clenched, the men labored. A radio played off to one side, blaring out rock music that did nothing to liven the mood. The men spoke little, concentrating on the work with grim determination.

Around noon there was a short break for lunch. A woman Petra hadn't seen before emerged from below. Quietly she moved along the deck handing out sandwiches and cans of cold soda. When she came to Petra, she nodded her head shyly.

"I'm Liz, Dave's wife. Sorry I didn't get up here before but the baby's been fretful."

Petra smiled at the young, slightly built girl. She was simply dressed in jeans and a T-shirt. Her light brown hair was caught back in a ponytail, and her slender face was liberally sprinkled with freckles. If she hadn't looked as worn as she did, she would have been pretty.

"I'd have come down to help if I'd known," Petra said. "I've just been taking pictures up here."

"Giles told us you take wonderful photographs," Liz said. "It's a pleasure to have you on board."

Petra grimaced slightly. She was used to people having the wrong idea about what her pictures would look like. "I'm not sure how wonderful they'll be," she said. "I try to catch what's really going on in a place." She hesitated a moment before she added gently, "Things seem pretty tough here."

Far from being offended, as Petra had feared, Liz nodded matter-of-factly. "Commercial fishing was never an easy life, but lately it's gotten a lot worse. Between the cost of fuel and help, the effects of pollution and the competition from foreign fishing boats, it's getting harder and harder to stay in business. But Dave is really determined. He worked other people's boats for ten years before he could afford *Windstar*, and he'll stick with her as long as he possibly can."

"What about you?" Petra asked. She itched to raise the camera and capture a portrait of Liz as she was at that moment—a young, tired, but obviously loving, woman on board a tough old boat surrounded by the endless, unforgiving sea. But she felt the woman's vulnerability and held back.

Liz shrugged. She brushed aside a strand of hair that had blown into her eyes. "I'll stick with him." She smiled. "I've got to check on the baby. Would you like to come below?"

Petra went gladly. In the tiny galley, where the pitch and roll of the boat could be most clearly felt, the two women chatted quietly. Nestled in a snug hammock that swung as securely as any cradle, three-month-old Davey, Jr., slept on. After a few minutes, Petra murmured, "Would you mind if I took some photographs?"

Liz was surprised. "Of us? Well, sure...if you really want to."

Petra smiled reassuringly. "I do, if it's all right with you. You both look so beautiful together."

Liz laughed. "I don't know about that. Davey's cute all right, but I look a wreck."

"No," Petra said quietly as she raised her camera, "you don't." She knew Liz didn't believe her. But later, when she saw the photographs, Petra was confident that Liz would realize what she had meant. There was a special beauty in the relationship of a mother and child that had nothing whatsoever to do with superficial details. In Liz's case, there was also a special poignancy, the tenderness of a mother who must prepare her child to cope with a world very different from the one she had hoped to give him.

The women were still talking when Giles came looking for Petra. His arrival in the small galley brought a sudden rush of male energy and strength, bursting the bubble of quiet female intimacy.

He looked from one to the other. "Is everything all right?"

"Fine," Petra said. "Liz and I have just been talking."

He was relieved that she seemed happy and relaxed. Bringing her along on the boat had been a risk. He'd known plenty of people—men as well as women—who would have found such an experience boring at best, if not outright distasteful. Petra, on the other hand, seemed to be in her element.

"I think I've gotten some good shots," she said as they went back up on deck. She had thanked Liz sincerely and promised again to send her the results.

"Then it hasn't been a wasted day?" he asked.

She shot him a quick glance. "No, did you think it would be?"

"I wasn't sure," he admitted.

Softly, almost under her breath, she smiled, "I'm not afraid of hardship. These people have it tough, but they deserve respect for that, not censure."

"What will you do with the photos?" he asked.

"I'm not sure. Right now, it's hard to say where they might lead, but they do seem to be a good antidote to the work I've been doing."

"What do you mean?"

She hesitated a moment before making up her mind. "When we get back, I'll show you."

## Chapter 4

The decision to show Giles her work hadn't been easy. Although she was a professional, taking photographs that were meant to be seen, she kept a cautious distance between herself and her audience. Not because she feared criticism—it was either helpful or it wasn't and nothing else counted—but because she was reluctant to reveal how much of her own soul was captured on the shimmering sheets of chemical-saturated paper.

Sometimes in the darkroom, when she pulled the prints still wet from the setting bath and hung them to dry, she would be struck by the sensation that a stranger had taken them, someone buried so deep within herself as to be barely perceptible. Yet someone who could make herself known all the same. Someone Giles might—or might not—like.

It shouldn't matter. She repeated that silently as she spread out a series of the black-and-white prints on the kitchen table. He was sitting directly across from her, his deep-set eyes watchful and attentive.

For a long time, he said nothing. His gaze swept over the photos again and again, coming to rest here and there, moving on, returning. Finally he sat back and looked at her, seated beside him.

"I knew I had heard your name somewhere. You've published several books. The *New York Times* ran a review of one of them that said you were one of a handful of photographers who would capture the sense of our age. Pretty heady stuff, but now I can understand it."

Petra blushed. It was an extraordinary and uncharacteristic response. She couldn't remember the last time she'd been embarrassed enough to show it. But this man—this strong, quiet, intelligent man—touched her in a way she had never before experienced.

"The *Times* reviewer is a friend of my agent's," she said by way of explanation.

He laughed reprovingly. "Which is supposed to mean that the article was biased? I don't buy it. You've got a very special way of looking at things."

He glanced down again at the photos. "Who's this?"

Petra looked at the young woman who had caught his eyes. She was about nineteen, blond—although that wasn't immediately obvious in the black-and-white photo. Her smile was soft and sensual, her eyes sharp. She had known she was being photographed but wanted to appear as though she did not.

"That's Cissy Dermott," Petra said. "Her father is Hugh Dermott. He made a fortune on leveraged buy outs. She goes to a lot of parties."

"What about this one?"

"Chas Fuller. He does group interaction art."

"What's that?"

Petra grinned. "He gets together with a bunch of his friends, they all put in ideas for what a painting should look like, then a guy who works for Fuller who can actually draw does the work. When the basic sketch is done, Fuller and his friends vote on what colors to use and the employee paints it."

"That stuff sells?" Giles asked skeptically.

"Like hotcakes."

He shook his head. "Maybe it's just as well I've been out of touch lately. Anyway, from what I can see, you're working on something that has to do with decadence in the upper reaches of what passes for society. Is that right?"

Petra leaned back. She was surprised by how quickly he had cut to the heart of it. Most people went on about her use of light and texture, her subtle shading, her distinctive way with focus, and so on. All baloney when you came right down to it, or at least not particularly important. What counted were the stark truths captured on the little pieces of paper.

"I don't make value judgments like that," she said slowly. "I just photograph what I see and leave the interpretation to others."

His eyebrows rose. "Are you telling me you didn't intend any of this?" He gestured to the photographs as though they were evidence in an indictment.

She shook her head. "I didn't get up one morning and say to myself, 'I think I'll go take some pictures of the useless rich to show everyone how awful they are.' I just thought it would be interesting to see what they revealed about themselves."

"What do they think of your photos?" Giles asked.

"That's the odd thing," Petra replied. "They keep inviting me to parties, and they go to all my gallery showings. It's horrible to say, but I think I've become fashionable."

Remembering her "gay, rambunctious" clothes, Giles smiled. "I thought you liked fashion."

"I do," Petra admitted. "But I've got a healthy-enough ego not to want myself put in the same category with a dress or a haircut."

Amused, Giles said, "Still, your agent must not mind it."

He glanced once more at the photos before turning his full attention to her. He saw a young, slender woman with innately graceful posture; a highly feminine woman in the best sense of the word. Someone who was strong, creative, interesting…and very, very desirable.

"Where will these photos be used?" Giles asked.

"They're for a book I'm doing," Petra said. Her breath caught. He reached out a lean, bronzed hand and took hers. With a gentle tug, he drew her to him. One moment she was sitting next to him, the next his iron thighs were beneath her bottom and she was ensconced on his lap.

"A book," he murmured. "That sounds interesting."

Flustered, Petra took a shaky breath. "W-what does?"

"The book." His breath was warm against her cheek. She felt the strength of his arms surrounding her with gentle firmness.

"Oh...it is...."

"There's so much about you that's...interesting...."His hard, seeking mouth brushed her slim throat. A shock of pure pleasure roared through her. She turned to face him as her hands closed convulsively on his powerful shoulders.

Breathless, teetering on the edge of capitulation so complete that it frightened her, she murmured, "Giles...is this a good idea...?"

She felt him smile against her skin. "Let's find out."

His mouth moved lingeringly along her throat to the lobe of her ear. She jumped as his teeth closed lightly before his tongue soothed away the infinitesimal hurt. Slowly, as though determined to savor every inch of her, Giles tasted her petal-soft skin. The feather-light touch of his mouth along her translucent eyelid sent tremors racing through her. Her lips parted with longing. She turned her head, meeting his mouth with hers.

So simple, a kiss. So devastating. Never had she known so complete an invasion of all her senses. Never had she dreamed she could so welcome it.

Heat pooled at the center of her being and radiated outward. She closed her arms around him, her fingers tangling in his thick, golden hair. She could feel the hammer-beat of his heart through her thin shirt.

Her eyes fluttered shut, the lashes casting long shadows over her flushed cheeks.

Timeless moments passed as the world faded into nothingness. Giles groaned deep in his throat. His hands stroked down her back to the curve of her hip and thigh. She trembled against him, driven by the desperate need to be even closer than they were.

Their tongues met and teased. She tasted the clean, minty flavor of him. He was all male power and tempered strength, certain where she was tentative, determined where she hesitated. The vague doubts she had nurtured about him were now revealed for what they were, a sham beneath which she had tried to take shelter from the incandescent male storm she had sensed was brewing just over the horizon.

Now it was exploding before her, sweeping her away in a tumult of emotions that both thrilled and terrified.

His hand moved across her flat abdomen, lingering with warm possessiveness. Her muscles tightened as wave after wave of yearning drove through her. He caught the back of her head, holding her still, as he deepened the kiss with relentless insistence. If there had been the slightest roughness, the faintest disregard for her feelings, she would have seized on it like a life raft and cast herself free of him. But he was infinitely gentle, infinitely giving, and she was left further and further at sea.

His fingers drifted up along her rib cage to settle lightly along the underside of her breast. Slowly his palm spread, cupping her as his thumb moved lightly over her hardened nipple.

A sob broke from Petra. She felt herself falling into a well of darkness from which there would be no escape.

A moment later she was free.

She straightened up slowly and stared at Giles. He was flushed, his eyes dark with barely restrained forces, his mouth a fiercely drawn line. She slid from his lap and stood up shakily, her hand braced on the back of a chair.

He also rose and left the table, walking a short distance away. With his back to her, he said, "Is that always how it is for you?"

Petra was baffled for a moment. He might as well have spoken in a foreign language for all the question meant to her. When she did understand, she sucked in her breath sharply.

"No," she murmured. "It...isn't." A wealth of meaning lay in those few words. It had never been anything remotely like that for her. She had never so much as imagined herself capable of such depth of feeling and need. The existence of such a hitherto unknown part of herself was terrifying yet oddly exhilarating. Life, it seemed, was even vaster and more mysterious than she had guessed.

"What about you?" she asked softly.

He laughed harshly. "Me? I thought I'd...been around, but it seems I was wrong." He didn't sound particularly pleased about that. Indeed, when he turned suddenly to confront her, his chiseled features looked as though they were cut from the hardest stone.

"As I said you are very interesting."

Talk about damning with faint praise. Petra was understandably stung. She looked away from him quickly. "I think you'd better go."

Her voice sounded stilted even to her own ears, but she couldn't help it. She was bombarded by conflicting feelings and impulses. Every instinct she possessed for self-preservation told her it was time to be alone.

Yet she had half expected him to insist on staying. Perhaps had half counted on it. Instead, he merely looked at her hard for several moments before abruptly turning away. When the door banged shut behind him, she stood trembling in the center of the room, her face ashen and her eyes bleak. All her life she had avoided such passions; now she knew why. They were unbearable.

Slowly she moved, straightening up the photographs in a mindless attempt to impose order on what would not be ordered. Carefully she tucked them away. When that was done, she sank down on the couch and put her head in her hands.

She did not cry, that release was denied her. But she stared for a long time at the impenetrable darkness behind her eyelids, trying to decide what to do.

He'd be a fool to see her again. That was it, plain and simple. To the best of his knowledge, he wasn't a masochist. He had absolutely no desire to embark on yet another relationship with a woman that would lead nowhere.

Amanda had not been an isolated incident. He had known other women whose objectives in life were so radically different from his own that they could never be reconciled. The trouble was, it had taken him thirty-two years to figure that out. It would be insane to start all over again.

If only knowing that meant something.

Sweet Lord, she was responsive. Also beautiful, young, intelligent, creative. A hell of a package.

But not for him. He wanted peace, a little tranquillity, a safe harbor.

He wanted a family.

A wife to start with, then children. Or he wanted nothing at all. He'd rather go it alone for the rest of his life than get involved in one of those modern relationships that either ended before it had barely begun or petered on for a few years until both parties got tired of picking pieces out of each other.

He wanted what didn't seem to exist anymore.

It had, once upon a time. He was convinced of that, no matter how naive it made him sound. With a sigh, Giles glanced toward the cases of books running along all four walls of the library. Aunt Emmeline had begun the collection, mostly with fiction, but the rest was his own. Many of the books dated from the late nineteenth century. To modern readers, they were wordy, boring and naive.

To him, they were a whole lot more.

He reached for one, touching the deep maroon binding gently. The pages were almost as crisp as the day they had been printed a hundred years before. Not like the books that were coming out nowadays with their high acid-content paper that self-destructed within a couple of decades.

These books had been written to last by a people who believed in permanence. They had believed in themselves, too. That, despite the upheaval of their world and the challenges coming at them right and left.

He smiled to himself. There was no doubt about it, the Victorians were a fascinating bunch. He'd been interested in them since childhood when he'd stumbled across the works of Sir Walter Scott, Conan Doyle and others. They'd been a refuge for him then. Maybe they still were.

That thought didn't please him. He scowled and wearily ran a hand through his hair. Off in the distance, a foghorn sounded. Giles glanced out the window. The beach beyond the stone walls had vanished. Tendrils of mist drifted through the garden. In another hour or so, the house would be socked in.

That was fine with him. He'd get some work done, have a light dinner, go to bed early. He'd forget all about Petra O'Toole with her glorious body, her fiery passion and her disturbing work.

He'd . . . fly to the moon.

Exasperated—with himself, the world, fate in general—he reached for the phone.

She wouldn't answer. Telephone rings were always supposed to be the same, but anyone with any sense knew that they weren't. The same telephone could sound perfectly ordinary and benign until something of genuine importance was about to happen. Then it sounded ominous.

Her hand shook. Petra glared at it and pulled the covers further up. The ringing would stop soon. She'd just stay here, safe and snug under the blankets, and ignore it until it went away. She shivered under the blankets. It wasn't cold, but she felt unaccountably weak, as though she might be coming down with something.

Two more rings. She shut her eyes, took a deep breath, told herself she absolutely shouldn't do this, and reached for the phone.

"I'm sorry," Giles said. His voice was deep and soft. It reached down through the phone line and wrapped itself around her heart.

"It's all right," she murmured.

"No, it isn't. I had no right to behave the way I did. At the very least, I owe you an explanation. Will you have lunch with me tomorrow?"

No, of course she wouldn't. She had far too much sense for that. Didn't she?

"Yes . . . I guess so. . . ."

She thought she heard a sigh of relief, but she could have been wrong.

"Good. I'll pick you up around eleven. Bring a swimsuit."

"All right. Giles . . . ?"

"Yes?"

"I think it would be a good idea if the two of us agreed . . . to just be friends."

He was silent for several moments before he said very gently, "Friends is fine, Petra."

She didn't know whether to be relieved or let down. Was it really that easy?

A moment later, she knew that it wasn't. His voice had a slight edge of purely male provocation, as he added, "For a start."

# Chapter 5

The beach was a golden crescent framed on either side by jagged rocks. Behind it lay a gentle crest of dunes, followed by a low stone wall and the green lawns of Great-aunt Emmeline's magnificent folly. Seabirds circled overhead. Off in the distance, a scattering of boats could be seen dimly through the lingering morning haze. Apart from them, Giles and Petra were alone.

The last time she'd gone to the beach, she'd been bored. This time she wasn't. On the contrary, she was vividly, achingly aware of the man stretched out on the blanket beside her. He lay on his stomach, his head resting on his folded arms and his eyes closed.

He was incredibly beautiful. There was just no other way to put it. Watching him through the heavy fringe of her lashes, she thought she had never seen a man who so perfectly epitomized what masculinity should be. He was muscular, but next to him muscular jocks would look clumsy and narcissistic. Even stripped down to a decorous swimsuit, he was elegant and sophisticated. All in all, he wasn't supposed to exist.

In her experience, he didn't.

Which, of course, didn't explain what he was doing lying beside her on the beach blanket, smelling faintly of suntan oil, his skin gently bronzed, his golden hair curling in the sea air, his warmth reaching out to touch her ever so tantalizingly.

Petra shut her eyes and stifled a groan. She was a grown woman, for heaven's sake, not some infatuated teenager with overactive hormones and a rampaging imagination. He was, when all was said and done, only a man. Except that seemed to mean more than she had ever guessed.

He was nice.

She hated that; she'd spent her life avoiding it. Nice was Norman Rockwell, apple pie, home and hearth, all that stuff that had been sold to her parents' generation and had long since turned up rotten in the sun.

Nice. Strong, safe, caring, fun, sexy. Oh, yes, very sexy. Enough to make her toes curl, which was such a cliché to start with but which actually happened when she looked at him.

Which she definitely should not be doing. He made her stomach clench, her heart race, her palms dampen. All those things she would have laughed at if they'd been happening to someone else. And she was a nice person.

Nice. There it was again. Run away from it as fast as you could and you'd find yourself staring right at it. She turned her head to the side and stared out over the empty beach. She could hear the sand whisper beneath her. Her ears were working all right; too bad the rest of her had turned to mush.

She wished she was different, more casual and insulated. Someone who—with the due care required these days—could get Giles Chastain out of her system by the simple expediency of going to bed with him. Once, twice, three times—how many would it take to exorcise him? In her case, she had the clear feeling that she didn't want to know the answer.

She was an idiot. She was also hot. Jumping up suddenly, she ran down the sand into the water.

Giles watched her go. He turned over on his side, his head propped on his elbow, his dark brown eyes turned to amber by the sun. Her body was perfect, slender and lithe, filled with sweet life. He wanted her desperately. Just thinking about how they would be together was enough to make him hard.

He smiled faintly. There was something to be said for reliving his adolescence. Something—not much. He was a man now, and yearning after a woman wasn't his style. Action suited him far better.

The water was pleasantly cool. He cleaved through it powerfully. Petra was out beyond the breakers. She saw him coming and stopped, treading water.

"Beautiful," she said.

"Yes," he agreed, "you are."

His mouth was hard, demanding. His arms were sleekly smooth with corded muscles and cool, wet skin. Their legs entwined beneath the surface of the water. She felt the brush of his desire and bit down hard on her lower lip to keep from saying then and there that she wanted him, damn whatever might come, and that they were fools to stay on an empty but public beach when they could be alone in a quiet room with the shades pulled down.

But she didn't. She tipped her head back to the sky, her hair trailing across the water, and stared at the floating, misty eternity above her. Nothing moved, nothing spoke, except for the distant foghorn that had been sounding long enough now to become barely noticeable.

Did people crash into rocks because of that? Did they hear the sounds of danger so often that finally they lost track of what they meant? Had she been so cautious all her life only to lose it all on a first, desperate throw of the dice? All for a prize she didn't dare understand?

"Giles..." she murmured on a thin thread of air, "remember what we talked about."

He raised his head, his eyes dark and slumberous with banked fires. "What was that?"

"Being friends."

He went very still, but he continued to hold her. Softly, almost sadly, he said, "I'm trying."

"So am I."

"There are even times when I think it's working."

"Me, too."

"And then," said Giles, "there are the times when I wonder why it's important. Men and women have been a lot of things to each other over the ages, but very rarely have they been friends. It hasn't been considered of much value.''

''It is to me,'' Petra said with quiet firmness.

His mouth twitched as a reluctant admission was wrung from him. ''It is to me, too. The problem is that I don't see being friends with you and desiring you as mutually exclusive. Sex can be very friendly.''

''I don't want sex,'' Petra said. She looked him straight in the eye. ''I've never been interested in that. What I would like is to make love with a good, strong, gentle man who also wants to make love with me. Is that so unreasonable?''

His throat was very tight. He was having trouble breathing, which was okay. Breathing was really extraneous in this kind of conversation. It had a life all its own.

Or at least he thought it did. He'd never been involved in anything like this before. But he recognized the feel of it. He'd read enough—and thought enough—to catch a glimpse of the souls of people who though long dead had left their passions behind them.

In a world that had still nurtured a proud innocence, they had believed in love. Enshrined it in their notion of the sacredness of family. Hallowed it in sacrifice, dying for it when they believed that was necessary. A hundred years ago—before nuclear bombs, toxic waste, drug-ridden cities and the like—there had been a world that, while far from perfect, had been founded on the notion of true, unabashed love. For family, nation, deity. Love that transcended all doubts and emboldened men and women to blaze a new course for humanity.

They'd been wrong about a lot of things, but the Victorians had been right about one—love was the most potent and fearful force in the universe.

And he'd fallen headfirst into it.

"Petra," he said softly.

Small white teeth released her lower lip. He saw a thin line of blood where they had been. Silently he vowed to find the most thorough way possible to erase that hurt.

"If we stay here much longer," he said, "sea gulls will make nests on us."

She laughed, nervously, but also with pleasure. "Do they do that?"

"All the time," he assured her solemnly. "It's a way of making people move on."

Her eyes met his. "I suppose that's what we have to do."

They swam side by side to the beach. Silently they toweled off and pulled their clothes on over their swimsuits. The sand was warm beneath their feet. They climbed over the stone wall and found the grass cool by contrast.

Hand in hand, carrying their shoes, they walked up the steps to the porch.

"Ouch," Petra said. She looked down quickly. Along the bare sole of her foot, a large, jagged splinter protruded. Already, the skin around it was turning red.

Without a word, Giles swept her into his arms. Effortlessly he carried her into the front parlor where he set her down gently on a horsehair sofa covered in red plush.

"Wait here," he said, "I'll be right back."

Before she could object, he was gone, only to return moments later with a damp cloth and a first aid kit.

"I'm sorry," he said gently as he knelt before her, "this will hurt for a moment."

If it did, she hardly noticed. The brush of his thumb along the arch of her foot was too tantalizing to allow for any other sensation. In a moment, he straightneed, holding the offending splinter aloft like a trophy.

"That's it. Feel better?"

She nodded, then watched as he brushed on a disinfectant and patted her foot dry. He was such a competent man, able and willing to take charge.

Which was fine when you needed a splinter removed but might conceivably prove inconvenient at other times.

"Leave your shoes off for a while," he said as he set her foot down gently. The carpet beneath was thick and soft. Her toes dug into it reflexively.

Giles was still kneeling before her. He looked up, his eyes meeting hers. Slowly, giving her ample time to pull away if she so wished, he moved his hand up along the curve of her calf, lingering at the soft inner cleft of her knee before lightly brushing the back of her thigh.

She swallowed with difficulty. Was it really so hot? No, it couldn't be. A soft sea breeze billowed the white lace curtains like gossamer sails. Sun shone through the mist. She could smell honeysuckle and the last dry remnants of the previous month's roses growing in tangled vines beyond the windows.

Then he moved, and she was aware of nothing except him.

It was too soon, they both knew that. They had met only a few days before. They had spent only a few hours together. There were significant differences between them.

Bed was no place to try to work out such things. It would only confuse the situation more.

Very clear, very calm, very . . . frustrating.

Giles clenched his fists. If he didn't stop touching her now, he wouldn't be able to stop at all. He wanted to strip her naked, lay her down on the soft, thick carpet and touch every inch of her. He wanted to see her back arch, her skin glow, her lips part in a moan of ecstasy. He wanted to feel her all around him, drawing him deeper and deeper into her mysteries, satisfying the terrible hunger only she provoked.

Madness.

"How about some lunch?" he asked.

Why not? If one primal need was impossible to fulfill, try another.

"I'll help," she murmured. Her legs felt very weak when she stood up. She decided that was because of the splinter and resolutely ignored it.

The kitchen was as she remembered—big, cheerful, neat. He took items from the refrigerator, laid out a wooden chopping board, and went to work.

"There's soup in the freezer," Giles said, not looking at her. "Would you mind warming it up?"

She found a large container from which the soup emerged like an immense frozen popsicle. Petra put it in a castiron pot, added a little water, and turned the burner on. She looked at the vegetables Giles was chopping.

"What are we having?"

"Chicken with scallions and peppers. The soup is made of ginger and turnips in chicken broth with hot pepper sauce. Is that all right?"

"It sounds wonderful," Petra said sincerely. She might not be much of a cook herself, but she liked to eat. She glanced at the implements he was working with—a small grater made of wood and resembling an intricately constructed screen, and a wide blade attached to a small handle for chopping.

"Did you get those in China?"

He nodded. "You can pick up just about anything you need right here, but I happened to bring these back with me." He didn't add that in those last, frantic hours before leaving Beijing, he'd packed only what could fit into a single small bag. Everything else—the jade figurines, the inlaid boxes, the books—had been left behind. With luck, his friends had gotten them. If they'd had the luck to still be alive.

There was so much she wanted to ask him about his experiences there and about his leaving. Usually she had difficulty containing herself when she was curious, but this time it was easy. Above all, she didn't want to hurt him.

They ate on the porch, seated at a table of wrought iron twisted into fantastic curlicues and painted white. The chairs were the same and would have been uncomfortable to sit in except that they were padded with deep plum-colored cushions.

The porch was set so that the breeze blew directly across it while the overhang of the house provided shade. An eminently sensible design. Petra found herself wondering why it had been largely abandoned in newer homes. But then so much else had been, too.

"This is delicious," she said, speaking softly so as not to interrupt the flow of peacefulness between them. It was a relief after the abbreviated passion, but it still couldn't fool her. The passion remained, hidden as though behind the mist, waiting for its own moment.

Its own, not whatever she or Giles might think was best.

"I'm glad you like it," he said. They were eating from plain blue and white bowls, with ivory chopsticks that lay on small ivory holders carved in the shape of fish. The holders, too, had been brought from China.

Petra touched one lightly. "When you came back, where did you go?"

"To Washington. I taught at Georgetown until a few months ago."

"What did you think of it?"

"It was . . . interesting."

She laughed softly. "That's damning with faint praise. I've been there a few times myself. New York thinks it has the lock on parties, but in Washington that's all anyone does."

He smiled, knowing she was right but wanting to tease her all the same. "What about Congress, the

Supreme Court, the Pentagon? Isn't that all serious business?''

"It's performance."

He shot her a quizzical look.

"Like that man I told you about, the one who does art with his friends. Oh, I know what goes on in government has much more serious consequences, but that doesn't mean the people involved are serious. They're too busy thinking about themselves, their own positions and prospects, to care much about the bigger picture.''

"You sound like a cynic," he said.

She looked at him, startled. "Well, of course I must be. I mean, isn't everyone? At least everyone I know.''

"In New York."

He made it sound like a tiny and very backward village that held nothing of interest.

"Look," she said, stung, "just because I don't harbor some silly romantic view of the world...."

"Yes, you do." She opened her mouth to protest, but he went on relentlessly. "You wouldn't take the photographs you do if you didn't want things to be different, better. You wouldn't have cared enough about Dave and the others to bother with them. You wouldn't show those society people throwing away their lives. You wouldn't need to be here.''

"It's just a vacation, for heaven's sake," she protested. "Not some kind of pilgrimage." For good measure, and because she was afraid, she added, "I'm not even sure I like it here.''

He shrugged. "What's that got to do with anything?"

She was dumbfounded. He should have been taken aback, at the very least, maybe even hurt. But then the thought of him hurt by something she had said hurt her, and she felt herself swept under by a current far stronger than herself.

"Forget it," she said. "Seriously, after you've seen the beach, appreciated the quiet—what there is of it—smelled the air and so on, what's so special about this place?"

"It's . . . cut off," he answered.

"The ferry runs at least eight times a day. There's also an airport."

"I know, but somehow that doesn't matter. It's separate, apart from the real world."

He smiled and raised his cup to her. "As you know, I was born in Hong Kong. Part of that is an island, the rest is mainland. I've come to believe that the inherent conflict between the two is responsible for much of the energy there."

"Energy?"

"In the soil, the rock. The Chinese call it '*feng shu*,' the spirit of the earth. In the old days, before anyone would put up a building, they'd bring the priests out to get the lay of the land, so to speak. They'd determine which way the intersecting lines of energy ran in the domain of the sleeping dragon. Sometimes, they'd say a place wasn't good for building at all. Oddly enough, a few years later, an earthquake would happen there. Somehow, those guys knew."

"Or managed to convince people they did," she said, dusting off her maligned cynicism. "I suppose that's all over with?"

He shook his head. "It's still common practice in Hong Kong. On the mainland, too, although they're more discreet. Smacks of religion, you see, which is supposed to have died away."

She speared a slice of pepper, chewed it, and said, "What would the *feng shu* priests make of this place?"

"Slippery. Much energy, but in flux."

"Should I brace myself for an earthquake?"

He leaned across the table and caught her hand with his own. "Only internally."

That was about as plain as it could be.

"Maybe," she said carefully, "I'm earthquake-proof."

He shot her a quick look. Was she saying what it sounded like? How could any woman filled with such incandescent passion know herself so little?

"And maybe," he said, "you shouldn't go through life filled with such misconceptions."

She cast him a chiding glance. "Are you offering to cure me of them, presuming they exist?"

He laughed, glad that he was too wise at least to fall into that one. "I would never be so presumptuous."

She looked at him for a long moment before she said, "Please pass the soy sauce."

## Chapter 6

When they were done, she helped him clear up. It seemed the decent thing to do even though a little voice in the back of her head told her to leave. This was more than she'd bargained for—much more. Her own wayward instincts were bad enough, but this man was playing for keeps. How she knew that, she couldn't say, but she was absolutely sure of it all the same.

But why with her? There was an extraordinary affinity between their bodies, but beyond that they had nothing. Couldn't he see that? He was domineering; she was independent. He was unapologetically old-fashioned; she was resolutely modern. He was committed to the past, she lived for the future. If they had anything at all together, it would be a very brief present.

She wasn't sure she could stand that.

She wasn't sure she couldn't.

Under the circumstances, there seemed like only one thing to do—have dessert.

"I shouldn't," she murmured as she lifted a forkful of chocolate torte. The cake was heavy, rich, smelling as though all the chocolate in the world had been poured into it. Before she took the first taste, she knew she was sunk.

It melted on her tongue. She closed her eyes for a moment, opened them again and saw Giles smiling at her.

"Chinese food is great, very healthy and all that. But sometimes you just have to have chocolate."

"Not sometimes," Petra said. "If I had my way, I'd eat chocolate morning, noon and night. I can't understand why I want it so much, but I do."

"It's a drug."

She laughed. "Sure it is."

"No, I'm serious. There is a chemical compound in it that scientists think gives the body a natural high. You like chocolate because it literally makes you feel good."

"Thanks," Petra muttered.

"Have another taste."

Their eyes met. Her mouth quivered. "Said the spider to the fly?"

He laughed again, very softly. "You're already in my parlor."

She stared at him across the expanse of white linen. He looked very big and hard in the filtered light. His shirt was of fine, well-washed cotton. Through it she could see the contours of his heavily muscled chest.

The shirt sleeves were rolled up. Fine golden hairs dusted his bronzed forearms.

"So I am," she murmured.

With the torte, he served a fine, slightly sweet champagne. Poured into fluted tulip glasses etched with gold, it danced pale and luminous as sunlight on a motionless sea. Petra took a sip, felt the effervescence rise within her, and decided this would be an opportune moment to excuse herself.

The bathroom was down a graceful hallway hung with bronze and copper wall sconces. At its end, she opened a heavy paneled door and stood, hands still on the knob, held motionless by delight.

Apparently Giles's willingness to ruthlessly redesign the kitchen with all the latest amenities had not extended to the bathroom. Here was Victoriana in all its unbridled glory.

Wainscoted walls glowed with the patina of decades. Above, they were papered with a pattern of blue-and-gray flowers twining along pale green vines. The tiled floor picked up the same colors. A pedestal sink and claw-footed tub were fitted with porcelain fixtures. Even the commode was in keeping with the mood, being royally encased in mahogany and with the water tank suspended high above near the ceiling. Plants were scattered all about in tubs and hanging baskets. A large bay window looked out at the garden and through a screen of trees, to the beach.

Petra splashed cold, clear water on her face. In the gilt-framed mirror, her eyes looked dark. This house, this blatant relic of the past, was growing on her by leaps and bounds. She thought of her own starkly utilitarian decor and winced.

"Everything all right?" Giles asked when she rejoined him.

"Fine, I was just feeling a little warm. That bathroom is fantastic."

He grimaced. "When I moved in here, a lot of things needed doing all at once. I hired a decorator to help me. She went a little overboard in places. It's authentic enough, just rather... frivolous."

"I would have said feminine," Petra demurred. "Do you think the two mean the same?"

Giles laughed. "Oh, no, you're not catching me on that one."

Her eyes danced. She took another sip of her champagne and looked at him over the rim of the glass. "Shucks."

"However, there are other ways...." He leaned over suddenly, closing the distance between them. His lips brushed her cheek. "Beautiful Petra," he murmured. His hand cupped the back of her neck beneath the heavy weight of her hair. "Like silk," he said as his fingers tangled in it. "Silk shot through with fire. It's not surprising that touching you makes me burn."

Her lips parted on a silent moan. He was so close, so commanding. She could feel reason sinking away. In another moment, it would be gone entirely.

"Who is the man?" he asked.

Her eyes flew open. She stared at him. "The what?"

"The man in the photographs." His voice was soft and gentle, yet with an iron streak of determination.

He would know; she would tell him. Whether she wanted to or not.

"I have no idea what you're talking about."

She tried to move away, but Giles did not release her. If she had pressed a little harder, he would have. That she did not, he took as a good sign.

"In the photos for your new book, there are six that show the same man. Tall, slender, very well dressed, dark hair and eyes, mid-thirties. He's the only person you photographed that frequently. Who is he?"

Petra was tempted to lie, to persist in claiming that she had no idea, but she couldn't bring herself to do it. Quietly she said, "His name is Daryl Ellis. He's an investment banker."

"Are you involved with him?"

"I was," Petra admitted slowly. "At least, I guess that's what you'd call it. Daryl and I spent some time together, that's all."

"He has no claim on you?"

Her mouth tightened. Firmly, making sure he didn't miss a word, she said, "No man has any claim on me."

A lambent fire showed in his eyes. "Really? Perhaps we should change that."

Arrogant, that's what the man was. A throwback to the days when man was king and woman was supposed to be glad of it. A creature from another era. An anachronism. However, he could kiss, she had to give him that.

Kiss long and deeply, sweetly and powerfully, until her senses whirled and she clung to him, fearful of being set adrift in a current she could not survive.

When at last they parted, he stood up quickly and moved away. From the distance of several feet, he said, "Petra, I've always been a cautious man."

Her eyebrows rose, dark slashes of russet across her brow. "Oh, really? I hadn't noticed."

His own uncertainty gave a sudden boost to her confidence. She rose and walked across the room. Standing in front of him, her hands resting on his broad chest, she said, "Going to live in China for three years wasn't very cautious. Neither was staying there after the trouble started. Or leaving what sounds like a good job in Washington to move to an island that most of the year is very quiet and remote. And then there's this house..." She smiled gently. "Most people would have wasted no time selling it. Instead, you decided to fix it up and live here. Not very cautious at all."

He smiled despite himself. She looked so serious and determined, as though she wouldn't let him think less of himself no matter what the consequences.

"All right," he said quietly, "then let's just say that I've bumped around a lot lately and it's made me a little wary."

Her eyes met his. "Was there a woman involved in this...bumping around?"

He thought briefly of Amanda, her cool, blond beauty and the life he would have had if he'd been willing to go along with her wishes.

"You could say that, but it was over before I came here. We didn't agree on what was important."

That was interesting, also safer than talking about Daryl. "What did she think mattered?" Petra asked.

She was genuinely curious. What would count with a woman attracted—and attractive—to Giles?

"Power," he said succinctly. "She envisioned me parlaying my China experience into a high-profile job at the State Department that in turn could be used as a springboard into politics." He laughed under his breath. "Believe it or not, I think Amanda has already decided how she'll redecorate the White House."

*"You're kidding?"*

"'Fraid not. The really scary part is that she just might pull it off."

"If she's so ambitious, why doesn't she go into politics herself?"

"Apart from the fact that her idea of a serious social issue is a seating plan for forty? Amanda's a realist. She knows that the kind of power she wants still belongs to men."

"That's baloney. Lots of women are winning elective office, and some of them are going straight to the top. Look at Margaret Thatcher."

"That's a different country."

"I know *that*. My point is that a woman can make it as far as she wants. We're held back only by our own insecurities."

"And other people's prejudices." Giles covered her hands with his own, holding them warm and protected against his chest. "It would be nice if the world was the way you describe it, Petra, but it isn't. There are still plenty of men who think women should be satisfied to be wives and mothers, and leave the important stuff to them."

"Being a wife and mother *is* important," Petra said stiffly. "What's more important than creating a family, looking out for each other, raising children? If we can't do that right, nothing else much matters."

His eyes narrowed, hiding his thoughts. "That's a singularly old-fashioned idea for someone who was arguing a moment ago for women being free to do anything they wanted."

"On the contrary, it's a thoroughly modern idea. Freedom means doing what really satisfies you deep down inside and doesn't hurt anyone else. For a lot of people—men and women—that means building something for the future."

"Did Daryl feel that way?"

She stopped dead and stared at him. Add sneaky to arrogant. "I didn't realize we were still on him."

"We aren't. We're on us. We're having one of those very modern conversations that men and women have to have these days before they do much of anything else. A clearing of the air, if you will."

Her mouth formed a small, perfect O. "One of those…"

"I thought you'd be completely up on that. Have everything on a flash card or something."

The implication that she had conversations of this sort routinely stung Petra. She pulled away from him.

"Why don't we just forget it?"

Giles laughed, not at all put out by her display of temper. He'd spoken clumsily and he knew it. But she scared him. She made him want things he thought he'd buried forever.

"I'm sorry," he said softly. "That was uncalled for. Jealousy brings out the worst in me."

Petra's eyes widened to luminous pools. "You're jealous of me?" she asked incredulously.

"Of Daryl," he corrected her. "Why do you find that so surprising?"

"Jealousy is an outmoded emotion. It suggests that somebody belongs to another person, whereas in fact we belong only to ourselves."

"Then you don't believe in exclusive relationships—monogamy and the like?"

"I didn't say that," she shot back, flustered. Please Lord, don't let them get started on monogamy. Next thing, he'd be talking about chastity, and that was definitely slippery ground.

"People can be faithful to each other," Petra insisted a little desperately, "without being possessive."

"And cows can jump over the moon. It's not part of human nature to deny ourselves anything we want without damn good motivation. The main reason people temper their sexual desires and remain faithful is because they want their relationship set apart from the rest of the world. They want it to be something exclusive and private, strictly their own. That's a basic human need that monogamy fulfills."

"What about morals?" Petra demanded. "What about ethics or religious teachings?"

"They're all an outgrowth of basic human needs," he insisted. "Many religions have preached monogamy because it's a good way of preventing conflict. Otherwise the strongest men tend to get all the women and the rest of the men tend to get revenge."

"It can work both ways, you know," Petra said. She was beginning to feel a little desperate. He described a world and a way of life that should have been repugnant to her, yet which she found oddly exicting.

Giles looked down at her gently. "It can, but usually it isn't. Men are different from women."

"Now there's a brilliant observation," Petra muttered. "The same one men have been using for thousands of years to justify all sorts of abuses. Different doesn't mean better."

"No," he agreed quietly, "It doesn't. It just means ... different."

As in iron strength against fluid softness; hard, masculine lips against silken skin; earth and sky bending toward each other. Petra never saw the arm that reached out and around her slim waist to draw her to him. Her gaze was caught by the sudden decisiveness of his expression, the light that glittered in his dark brown eyes, the realization that the time for talking was over.

Her body arched against his, fluid and supple. They kissed hotly, lingering on the taste of each other, their bodies moving restlessly. His hardness against the chalice of her hips sparked deep tremors of need. Her breasts rubbed achingly against his chest. Her nipples were acutely sensitive. She felt herself melting within as her body obeyed commands older than time and far beyond the reach of reason.

And all the while the curtains fluttered, the old house whispered softly around them, and the mists clung, hiding them from the world, creating a world of their own.

Upstairs in the bedroom, the hushed sense of separateness was complete. Cradled in Giles's arms, Petra tried hard to catch hold of her whirling senses. The room was shaded by the branches of an ancient oak tree. Heavy velvet drapes hung at the high windows. A marble-manteled fireplace glinted whitely against paneled walls.

In the midst of the room, facing the fireplace, stood a magnificent sleigh bed that even Petra, with her lack of knowledge about antiques, recognized as choice. It was covered with plain white sheets and a simple white comforter that stood out in stark contrast to the opulence of their surroundings.

The comforter was cool behind her back. Her hair spilled over the pillows, red and gold against the white. Giles bent above her, his knee pressing into the mattress, his face taut.

"Petra...are you sure...?"

Her mouth was very dry. It took an effort to answer. She wished he wouldn't insist on that. It would be so much easier to just let herself be carried along. But Giles demanded more.

"Yes," she murmured on a thread of sound, "I'm sure."

She was lying. She knew it as certainly as she knew anything at that moment. The mere idea that she could be sure of what she was about to do was absurd. If she'd been in a clear mental state, she would never have gotten as far as the bedroom. But she was—how did the old song go—bewitched, bothered and bewildered. Which, all things considered, seemed pretty good.

Sometimes a woman had to take a risk. Throw caution to the wind. Go with the flow. All that stuff. She'd spent her whole life being safe and sure, and where had it gotten her? Fabulous career, okay. But she could tell anyone who cared to listen that no camera kept her warm at night, or staved off the loneliness that too often plagued her.

She wanted to be touched. She wanted to be set soaring. She wanted to obliterate all the doubts and the fears, the hesitations of everyday existence.

For once in her life, she wanted to do something flat-out crazy.

Which was fortunate, because that was exactly what she was about to accomplish.

With Giles's help.

Oh, he was good at it. So very, very good. She spared a moment to think of the experiences that had made a professor of British history, a fan of the Victorians, so potent in bed. But that really didn't bear thinking about. Better to concentrate on how he made her feel.

As though she was melting.

Disturbing but delicious. Like ice cream puddling along the edges of the dish. Soon the center would go all mushy. Soon there would be nothing to do except spoon her up.

Was it supposed to be like that? She hadn't the foggiest, nor did she really think it made a difference. Now was now, and nothing else much mattered.

Her clothes slipped away as though they had never been. She felt the cool brush of air against her skin and stretched luxuriously. A secret, seductive smile curved her mouth.

Giles paused, hand on the zipper of his fly. He was hard as a boy and as precarious in his self-control. That was a new experience for him. He'd always prided himself on never quite letting go of rationality. Now he couldn't quite remember what that was.

Hastily he disposed of the final barriers between them and joined her on the bed. Her skin was impossibly soft, her body incredibly lovely. His hands wandered over high, firm breasts, a slim waist and hips, long, sculpted thighs. Her naval was a dimple in the midst of paradise. He dipped his head and tasted her there, causing her to cry out and curl inward self-protectively as though the pleasure was too much to bear.

He laughed, a deep, utterly masculine sound that conveyed a wealth of information about his intent to master her, not to mention his confidence that he would do so. Meeting the challenge of it, Petra unwound and faced him defiantly.

"Let me," she whispered as she touched her mouth to the hard corded muscles of his chest, tracing them downward along the ridge of his ribs to the line of golden hair that crossed his abdomen before burgeoning at his groin. That far she didn't dare to go. Slowly she retraced her steps, pausing to lick the turgid male nipples before burrowing her head into the hollow of his neck as shyness overcame her.

"For God's sake," he muttered, "don't stop now."

When she remained still and silent in his arms, he turned her over gently and looked at her.

"Petra...is something wrong?"

"No," she told him shakily. "I'm just not...all that used to this."

He shot her a look combined of confusion and incipient understanding. "But I thought..."

"Daryl and I were just friends."

He found that incredible to believe but was willing to let it go for the moment. "What about before him?"

"I've...always been very busy."

Giles froze. What exactly was she telling him? It sounded as though she meant that she'd never... No, that was impossible. No woman as beautiful and seductive as Petra could possibly have reached her mid-twenties without ever going to bed with a man. Could she?

But if, by some almost unbelievable set of circumstances, she had somehow remained a virgin, he should at least have the decency to draw back now before things went any further.

Giles's battle with his conscience was as brief as it was intense. In the end, uncounted generations of Norman-Saxon ancestors rose up to tell him, in the plainest possible language, not to be a flaming idiot. If a man had something as rare and precious as this woman handed to him, he damn well made the most of her. He did not—repeat not—leave her sitting around waiting for some other, smarter man to come along and take what should have been his.

Decency had nothing to do with it. That would come later.

The smile that curved his mouth held everything of conquest and nothing at all of doubt.

"Petra, have I told you how beautiful you are?"

"You hinted a time or two."

"I couldn't possibly have done you justice. Words are inadequate. However..."

He proceeded to show her, in the most thoroughly possible way, leaving no room for doubt, let alone any energy. All she could do was breathe—more correctly, gasp—and cry out as the undulating crests of pleasure carried her higher and higher into a realm where the air was very thin and the light almost unbearably bright.

Then the light was inside her and all fear was gone. Whatever pain there had been was forgotten before it occurred. There was only Petra and Giles, united in the rarest and most complete of bonds. All barriers down, all fears dissolved. Two halves of the same whole finding each other.

Until the earth re-formed beneath them, and the reality of what they had shared had to be faced.

Petra shivered and pulled the sheet up over herself. Giles lay beside her, his broad, sun-bronzed chest rising and falling, a real, living, breathing man who had just possessed her more completely than she would ever have believed possible.

And who looked damn satisfied with the experience.

She shivered again when his eyes opened and he looked straight at her. Clearly, without thinking how it would sound, he said, "You certainly are full of surprises."

## Chapter 7

The last I heard," Petra said stiffly, "it wasn't a crime to be a virgin."

"Don't be silly," Giles muttered. He was handling the situation badly and knew it. The problem was he couldn't seem to help himself. His usual careless grace with women had deserted him.

"No one's suggesting it's a crime," he went on, willing himself to patience. "However, you will admit it is surprising in this day and age."

Petra flushed. Still struggling to come to terms with what had happened between them, she was in no mood to be reminded of her own failure of honesty.

Abruptly she said, "I hate postmortems. They're boring and pointless."

Before he could reply, she left the bed, grabbed the comforter to cover herself and began gathering up her clothes.

Giles lay on his side, propped up on his elbow, watching her. The sheet was pushed down to his hips. His long, lean body glowed darkly in the pale light. A scowl creased his forehead.

"What do you think you're doing?"

"Leaving."

For a moment, she thought he wasn't going to answer. She didn't dare turn around to see what he was thinking, and she wasn't about to ask him. All she wanted was to get out of there as quickly as possible.

Until the hard, heavily muscled arm lashed out, and an iron hand gripped her arm.

"Let me explain something to you," Giles said as he unapologetically dragged her back to the bed. "There's a certain etiquette to all this, of which you are apparently ignorant. Under the circumstances, I can excuse that. However, it's time you broadened your horizons."

"W-what do you mean?" Petra gasped. She lay flat on her back, still clutching the comforter and her clothes. Giles loomed above her, his face oddly tender in contrast to his words.

"It's very rude to walk out on your lover," he growled softly. "It's liable to lead to all sorts of hurt feelings and misunderstandings. So why don't we just avoid all that? You and I need to talk. This is as good a place as any."

"No," Petra said emphatically. Inexperienced she might be; stupid she wasn't. "I'm not staying here with you." The light in his eyes suggested she had better rethink that double quick.

"We can talk downstairs," she suggested, trying to sound reasonable and mature. "And by the way," she added for good measure and because she wasn't about to let him get the upper hand, "while it may be rude to walk out on a lover, it is also worse than rude to detain someone against her will. Kindly let go of me."

He waited just long enough to make the point that he was going along with her because he wanted to, not because she said to. He released her, and without another word tossed the sheet aside and got out of the bed. Standing stark narked, feet planted slightly apart and hands on slim hips, he smiled down at her.

"Okay, let's go."

Petra tried her best to look anywhere but at him, only to find that her eyes seemed to be glued. Desperately she demanded, "Not until we're both dressed."

His smile widened. "In that case, I'd just as soon stay here."

"Not a chance," Petra said. She scrambled off the other side of the bed and marched into the adjacent bathroom. "You've got five minutes, Chastain. If I were you, I'd make the most of it."

Once the bathroom door closed behind her, her bravado vanished. She slumped against the sink, avoiding looking at herself in the mirror, and drew several deep breaths. They didn't help. Her hands were shaking as she pulled on her clothes, then ran her fingers through her hair in a futile effort to return it to some semblance of order.

Only then did she steal a glimpse of herself. Her skin was very pale and her eyes looked unusually dark. By contrast, her lips were red and there was a slight abrasive mark near the hollow of her throat. She looked like a woman who had been well and truly loved. Worse yet, she felt like one.

The bedroom was empty when she slipped back in. The door to the hallway stood open. Petra walked gingerly down the long, carpeted hallway to a curving mahogany staircase. Light poured onto the landing through a magnificent stained-glass panel portraying a woman holding a basket from which grapes spilled. Behind her, a bucolic country scene vanished into the distance.

Petra shook her head dismally. She hadn't even noticed the stained glass as Giles carried her up the stairs. Truthfully she hadn't noticed anything at all. The world itself might as well have ceased to exist when she was with him.

Which was utterly ridiculous—no sane person could live like that. She was going to put a stop to it right now.

He was waiting for her in the kitchen. As a concession to her modesty, he'd put on a threadbare pair of shorts but nothing else. As he finished spooning coffee into the pot, he glanced over his shoulder and said, "Feeling better?"

"Oh, sure," she muttered. "There's nothing like being in free-fall to give a girl a lift."

"Is that where you've been?" He laughed softly. "I've heard some interesting descriptions of it, but that..."

He broke off and came over to her. Standing very close, he brushed her cheek with the back of his hand. "Seriously, you're all right?"

Feeling her cheeks heat, she nodded her head. "I'm fine. I appreciate your concern, but there's no need. Look, I really have to get going."

His hand dropped away, but otherwise he did not move. "Why?"

"I still have pictures to develop for my new book. This was supposed to be a working vacation, and I'm way behind. All of the rest—of us—was an accident. These things happen, I realize that, but there's no reason to let it get control of us. After all, we both have our lives to live."

Giles was a man of silences, she was beginning to realize. Silences that spoke reams about what he was thinking. She could hear a clock ticking in the background.

It seemed to go on for a long time before he said, "I see . . . You're sure that's what you want?"

Not remotely. But having gone this far Petra didn't see how she could turn around. The whole thing had gotten out of hand. She felt horribly inadequate, a sensation she had known only too well as a child and had struggled to suppress ever since. Now it was back with a vengeance. She had to struggle even to breathe.

"Yes," she murmured, forcing herself to look straight at him, "that's what I want."

Slowly, with obvious reluctance, Giles stepped aside. They stared at each other for several moments before Petra jerked her head away. The back door was only a few feet away. She had to force herself not to run for it.

Giles lay back in the hammock and looked up at the leafy arch fluttering gently above him. Somewhere nearby a catbird sang, its mocking cry a reminder that no man's ego was sacrosanct.

Certainly not Giles's. His was well and thoroughly dented. All his past experience with women had flown out the door right along with Petra herself. Maybe it would be good for him in the long run. Sort of like a tonsillectomy.

Who was he kidding? Losing Petra was a hell of a lot harder than anything he'd yet experienced. China had been terrifying and infuriating, but he'd been one among hundreds of millions, and no matter how bad things got, he'd had his own country to come home to. This was different.

No other woman had ever touched him in the way Petra did. She took him out of himself, made him part of something far larger, yet also made him feel unaccustomedly humble. Perhaps it was that experience of being both smaller and yet more worthy than he had ever imagined that made him so determined to hold on to her.

She gave him a new sense of perspective—and more possibilities—than he had thought possible. Amanda had never had that effect, nor had anyone else. He'd always held something back, wary of committing himself to what simply wasn't right. With Petra, he was in up to his neck, and the water was rising fast.

He uttered a low curse as he got out of the hammock and walked swiftly back to the house. Trying to think it out would get him nowhere. He needed good, hard action to quiet his mind and let his reason work.

Dave provided it. Word was that the tuna were running, so despite the late hour and the lack of an adequate crew, *Windstar* would sail. Giles made it on board scant minutes before the lines were cast off. He spent the next ten hours sweating and straining with half a dozen other men as they fought to capture some of the most magnificent animals the sea has ever produced.

Going for tuna under an iridescent moon was an experience not to be missed. It was also hard, grinding work that demanded absolute concentration. Giles had always loved the sea best at night, but he had also always understood that it was never more treacherous. Men were creatures of the land and the day. They trespassed at their own peril.

In the end, when the wind was running high and they were fighting exhaustion, Giles sat in the galley with Dave, nursing a steaming mug of coffee. Liz was on shore along with the baby. The other men were on deck, taking their own hard-earned breaks.

"Good catch," Giles said quietly.

Dave shrugged. "So far. We probably lost a few with the new nets."

"Any second thoughts about that?" Giles asked.

Dave shook his head. "I never liked it when we'd go for tuna and end up with dead dolphins. Didn't seem right somehow. With the new nets they can get away."

"Along with a few of the tuna."

"Those are the breaks." Dave smiled wryly. "If we ever end up talking to those dudes, I don't want to have to explain what happened to their grandpas."

"I agree with you," Giles said, "but it makes things tougher for you."

Dave shrugged. "Life is tough. You must have figured that out by now." He paused for a moment before he said, "How's Petra?"

Giles grimaced. "Okay, I guess."

"The two of you have a fight?"

"Not exactly, more of a misunderstanding." A doozy of one.

"Liz liked her. Said she was real."

Real? A woman who remained a virgin until twenty-six and then fled after her first sexual encounter, which by all admission had gone very well but still hadn't been enough to overcome whatever deeply seated inhibitions held her in thrall. That was real, all right. It was also damn hard to deal with.

"She's a good photographer," Giles said. "Better than that even."

"It's okay for women to work," Dave said magnanimously, "long as that doesn't get in the way of the important stuff."

Giles laughed outright. "Don't let Petra hear you say that, or a whole lot of other women for that matter."

Dave's weather-beaten face creased self-consciously. "Liz is always on me about that. She says I'm a troglodyte, whatever that is."

"A fossil left over from prehistoric times. Yeah, that sounds right."

"So I don't go in for a lot of flashy trends," Dave asserted. "Listen, before the baby came, Liz was out on this boat every single day. And before that, when we were saving to go on our own, she held down two jobs, same as me. But now things have changed. She's got a baby to look after. Yeah, we could use more money, but what good is it if our kid ends up trashed?"

Trashed. Kids. Petra had said her parents were divorced. She'd glossed over it, but he'd gotten the definite impression that there'd been more than she was willing to tell. Now he regretted not having followed up when he'd had the chance. If he had, it was hard to tell with her. Daryl notwithstanding—some wimp he must be—she'd clearly spent years avoiding intimacy of any kind. When finally confronted with it, she'd run for her life.

He was going to have his work cut out for him, Giles realized. Especially since he was no great shakes at that intimacy stuff himself. They'd just have to learn together.

"Thanks, Dave," he said quietly.

The other man raised his eyebrows. "What for?"

The way the question was asked, laconically and with a little grin, gave Giles the definite impression that Dave knew perfectly well why he was thanking him. But he said only, "I needed to clear the air. No better place to do that than a boat."

"That's for sure," Dave agreed. "Nature has a great way of making sure you know what counts and what doesn't."

Nature also had a great way of wearing you out. By the time Giles returned home, it was early morning. He was more than tired; fatigue had numbed him so that he barely felt the aching of his body and the hollowness of his heart.

He stood under the shower for a long time, letting the hot water sluice over him until the old boiler finally sputtered and the water turned cool.

With a towel wrapped around his hips, he cleaned the mist from the mirror and thought briefly about shaving. Deciding against it, he padded barefoot down to the kitchen. His stomach was empty, but nothing in the refrigerator looked appealing. He shrugged and decided he needed sleep more than food.

He was heading back upstairs when the soft crunch of gravel drew him up short. He glanced out the window, beyond the billowing white lace, and froze.

Through the salt-misted panes of glass, draped in the shadows of the porch, Petra gazed back at him.

It hadn't been easy, deciding to go back to the fantasy house perched near the dunes and act like an adult for a change. But a long, sleepless night and an equally long talk with herself had forced Petra's hand. There came a time when a woman had to do what a woman had to do, even if it meant admitting that she had acted badly.

Of course, it would have helped if he'd had some clothes on.

Was there some immutable reality in the universe that decreed she should be thrown totally off balance just when she needed all the help she could get?

*Let's see how she reacts to this one,* Fate said, chuckling.

"Hello, Giles." The voice was a little husky but otherwise okay. She even managed a faint smile that lasted for about half a second.

"Hello, Petra." He sounded skeptical, wary and not particularly welcoming.

She took a deep breath. "Do you think I could come in?"

He didn't answer directly, but he did walk to the front door and open it. Standing framed in the entry, a bronzed male body lightly covered by a white terry cloth towel, he looked at her challengingly.

"I didn't expect to see you here."

"Yes, well . . . I didn't really expect it myself." He made no effort to stand aside and she could hardly push her way past, so she stood, arms akimbo, looking at him.

That wasn't hard to do. His thick golden hair was matted to his head. His eyes were deep set; he looked tired. A wave of doubt washed through her.

"I shouldn't have bothered you."

"But you have, so you might as well stay." He moved back a few inches, enough to let her by but not enough to concede much else.

She squeezed past and stood in the dimly lit hall fragrant with lemon oil, her hands clenched and her nerves on end.

Staring down at the Oriental rug with its magical, mystifying design, she said, "I'm sorry."

Giles shut the door. The sound reverberated against the old mahogany paneled walls. He turned and looked at her. "What for?"

She laughed nervously. "For being an idiot? I don't know, exactly. But I do know I behaved badly. I shouldn't have run off the way I did."

He softened. She actually saw it happen, saw the relaxing of tension from his hard, masculine features. Saw the beginning of forgiveness—and acceptance.

Saw that they had been there all along.

"It's all right," he said quietly.

"No." She was emphatic, gaining confidence from the realization that he didn't despise her. And all the implications of that.

"It's not all right," she said. "I'm really sorry."

She didn't look like a little girl.

That sunk into him, not slowly but like a sharp, hot knife cutting through butter.

She could very easily have looked childlike, standing there with her hands together and her head ducked. But she still looked like a grown woman. She wasn't trying any of the "little girl" moves that women sometimes resorted to when they were being particularly manipulative. She was playing it straight.

He allowed himself a small sigh of relief that concealed a vast sea of the same. "Want some coffee?"

She looked up quickly, catching him before he could guard himself. "Yes."

She sat at the kitchen table while he made it. When the pot was perking, he excused himself and went upstairs to put some clothes on. By the time he returned, dressed in khaki pants and a cotton sweater, the coffee was ready.

They took it out on the porch. At this quiet hour of the morning, the air was scented with honeysuckle and salt. The two might have canceled each other out, but instead they made an oddly pleasing combination.

Petra sat down in a white wicker rocker padded with cushions Giles had brought from the house, where they stayed nice and dry during the dew-drenched nights. He paid attention to details; not much got past him.

"You're being very nice about this," she said softly.

"I have a vested interest."

Her grip on the cup tightened. "What's that?"

"I . . . care a lot about you."

Tears burned her eyes. She blinked them back hastily. "Thank you. I care about you, too."

"Good," he said with a smile. "Since we've established that, where do we go from here?"

"I . . . need to explain something to you—a problem I have."

"Getting close to people."

Sapphire eyes shot open. "Oh, great. Is there anything you haven't already figured out?"

He shrugged unapologetically. "I'm a historian. That means my business is people, how they behave and why. You told me your parents were divorced when you were a kid. My guess is that you ended up pulled between them. It doesn't take a genius to figure out what that meant."

Petra looked at him cautiously. Her voice was low and quiet as she said, "Lots of kids go through worse."

"We're not talking about lots of kids. We're talking about you."

Which made it pretty hard to equivocate, although she was certainly tempted. This business of having to be frank with somebody was new to Petra. She was used to reserving her honesty for her work.

She had no camera now, nothing to hide behind. And she had come of her own volition, no one had forced her. Slowly she said, "My parents were always asking me if I loved them. Every time I went to one or the other, they wanted to know where they stood. It was a competition between them."

"What did you say?" Giles asked gently. He had sat down in the wicker settee next to her. His long legs were stretched out. He appeared at ease, but she knew the appearance was deceptive. She could feel his attentiveness.

"I tried not to say anything, but after a while I ended up saying 'yes.' 'Yes' to everything and nothing, just to make them stop. It got to the point where I hated saying 'yes' at all."

"You said 'yes' last night by staying here, and you said 'yes' again by returning."

"I know," Petra said faintly. "It wasn't easy."

"Why did you?"

"I . . . don't know."

He laughed. "You're hard on a guy's ego, you know that?"

"I'm sorry," she murmured.

"Hey," he said quickly, covering her hand with his own, "I'm just kidding. I'm a grown-up, I can take it."

"You shouldn't have to. You're . . . wonderful."

He sighed. "I'm a man, Petra, that's all. Let me tell you what you're dealing with here. I didn't sleep at all last night. After you left, I stewed around for a while before realizing I was going nowhere fast. So I called Dave and went out on the boat. We were out all night. Took in a pretty good haul of tuna, but that's beside the point. The only way I got this far was by wearing myself out, plain and simple."

"I'm sorry," she whispered, appalled by what she was hearing. She'd had no idea that he would be so affected.

"That's not the point. You're vulnerable, but so am I. I'm very attracted to you. You're beautiful, intelligent and talented. But you've also been hurt. I'd like to think we could get past that."

"What about you?" Petra asked thickly. She was trying very hard to stay composed, but it didn't come easily. "Your parents died. All mine did was get a divorce."

"I hardly knew my father," Giles said, "and without wanting to sound callous, I had plenty of uncles who were only too happy to take his place. I never lacked for a father's influence. As far as my mother went, she was just an image to me, somebody who showed up in the nursery dressed to go out and smelling good. Nice, but not what you'd call necessary. Even before she died, one of my aunts had taken me in hand. I guess I still really think of her as my mother.''

"You were lucky," Petra said quietly.

"I know." Giles meant it. To the depths of his being, he recognized his good fortune. "I was never pulled in two."

"Like saltwater taffy," Petra said with a smile. "That's how I thought of it. The problem is, I like saltwater taffy. I eat it every chance I get."

"You have terrible taste," said Giles, the purist.

"No," Petra said gently, looking at him. "I have exquisite taste."

He was embarrassed, as any man might be by such a compliment.

"I wish," he said fervently, "that I wasn't so tired."

But he was. Reality had a way of catching up with thirty-two-year-olds. He'd been up all night, hauling in three hundred pound tuna. Whatever ideas his mind might have, his body had other priorities.

"I didn't get any sleep, either," Petra said with a smile. Daringly she added, "Let's go to bed."

Between crisp, cool sheets scented with salt air, they slept. Twined together, their bare bodies browned by the sun, they lay in easy unconsciousness through the long, drifting afternoon. Sea gulls turned overhead, flowers opened and closed, all around them the world went about its business. They slept, safe and secure as children.

And woke to the joyful knowledge that they were more.

## Chapter 8

The taste of sun and earth lingered on Petra's tongue. She swallowed the freshly picked blackberry and held out her hand for another.

"They're delicious," she said.

"They're supposed to be for a pie." The reprimand was gentle. Giles had already eaten his share of the berries and then some.

"They're better this way," Petra insisted. Carefully she slipped her fingers between the thorns and plucked another, popping it into her mouth. "Much better."

"We could go back to the house," Giles suggested. "We could cover them with cream, sprinkle on a little sugar, eat them off silver spoons or..."

"You're terrible," Petra protested, laughing. "Look at this." She held out her arm. "See how pale I am. Can you guess why that is?"

"Lots of sun block?" he inquired innocently.

"I've hardly been outside in a week." She leaned closer to him, eyes dancing. "Somebody—I won't say who—has been keeping me inside, in a cool, shadowy room with a very large bed."

"Terrible," Giles murmured. He picked a particularly nice blackberry and popped it into her mouth. "I don't know how you could stand it."

Petra giggled, a singularly unusual sound for her. "I don't know how I survived it. There was many a time when I thought I was just absolutely going to perish."

"Was there?" Giles grinned. He touched his lips to hers, communicating a sweetly evocative taste. "You must tell me all about it. Or better yet, show me."

"Right here?" she asked with feigned innocence. "What about the thorns?"

"Good point," he said with alacrity. "We've got enough berries."

Petra glanced down at the scant cup or so that had survived their maraudings. "We do?"

"Don't you know pie is fattening? Let's go."

She agreed, laughing. She seemed to do a great deal of that these days. Life had taken on a carefreeness that was new to her; she suspected it was to Giles, too.

In the week since she had faced her fears and determined to conquer them, they had been together almost constantly. Mornings were spent bicycling around the island. They visited the bluffs where decades of erosion had taken crescent bites out of the land. On a particularly cool morning, they rode to the edge of Rodman's Hollow and hiked in, spending several hours wandering through untouched land where the silence was so complete they might have been in another world.

Afternoons were devoted to sinfully rich lunches, followed by siestas. Waking, they turned instinctively to each other. In the height of the day, when insects buzzed outside windows shaded by striped awnings, they made love. Time did not exist; there was never any reason to hurry. Day flowed into night into day with seamless rhythm. For the first time in her life, Petra came to understand what it meant to be content.

It was a fragile emotion, brittle as fine bone china, and deserving of protection. She tried her best even as she sensed that the bruising world was merely lying quiet, not gone away forever.

She had taken to wearing dresses, long, flowing white cotton ones that she found at the cavernous general store on Water Street. They were hung at the back of the store, bearing labels reading Made in India, but looking as though they had been merely forgotten from another era.

She dried them on the line behind Giles's house, since she was rarely at her own. They emerged stiff, as though they had been starched, and smelling of the sun. After an hour or so on her body, the smell lingered but the stiffness was largely gone.

The humidity turned her hair to a riot of curls that overcame any comb. She thought of cutting it but relented when Giles spent an imminently satisfying hour demonstrating his fondness for the red-gold mass. She compromised by catching it up in mock tortoiseshell combs so that it framed her face like a lazy, drifting cloud.

Despite her protestations, her skin was not pale but golden. All over. Because during the week, when the tourists were minimal, Giles knew a particularly secluded stretch of beach where swimsuits seemed superfluous.

The first time he coaxed her into shedding her inhibitions about nude swimming, she had been nervous and self-conscious. But the experience was curiously liberating. Now she was as likely as he to suggest that they head for their special place.

Not that day, however. It was Saturday, which meant that the island was crawling with day-trippers who came over on the ferries from Point Judith or New London. Petra supposed it was unfair to look down on them since some were perfectly nice people. But there was also a high percentage of yahoos who liked nothing better than climbing up on a moped and seeing how many traffic laws they could break.

Given her own brush with moped-engendered disaster, Petra gave the vehicles a wide berth. She was relieved when they arrived back at Giles's house where they could figuratively raise the drawbridge and shut out the rest of the world.

But not entirely. She'd told him the truth about needing to work while she was on the island, and she was now even further behind schedule than before. When she'd finally admitted that a day ago, he'd come up with the obvious solution.

"Why don't you bring the photos over here? You can work on them while I do some writing. I'm a little under the gun myself."

He'd finished the page proofs for his new book, she learned, but he was due to turn in the manuscript on the next in less than four months. There was still a great deal to do on it.

"What are you writing about?" Petra asked.

"The same, labor issues in Victorian England."

She did her best to look interested, which prompted a chuckle. "It's not as bad as it sounds. Actually it was a fascinating time, filled with conflict and high emotion. Moreover, what those people went through trying to cope with the industrial age has a certain amount in common with what we're going through with post-industrialism."

"Post-industrialism. Is that where we are? Industrialism doesn't seem to have lasted very long." History wasn't her strong suit, and she was always rusty on dates, but she had the idea that the industrial revolution had happened just a couple of centuries ago.

"On a scale relative to the whole of human existence, it rates a long weekend, maybe a little more. But it had a tremendous impact, and so will the move away to a more service-oriented, technological society."

"It doesn't seem fair somehow," Petra mused. "People no sooner get used to one way of life than it changes."

"That's the problem, all right. People right now are almost shell-shocked by the pace of change. But they were then, too. We can read letters and diaries in which perfectly intelligent, sensible people speculated that the end of the world was at hand.''

''And they didn't even have nuclear weapons,'' Petra mused.

''No, but they were already beginning to poison their environment, and toward the end of the age they began to realize it. The more people piled into cities, the worse the air and water became, the more people died from them. The trouble was that the rich and powerful could always escape, so they lacked an incentive to clean up their act.''

''And now,'' Petra said softly, ''there is no escape.''

Giles nodded. He looked around at the curving rise of the hill dotted with tangles of blackberry bushes and the occasional trampled patch where deer had passed through.

''Maybe that's good,'' he said. ''Something is finally getting done, at least here. Unfortunately the developing countries seem determined to repeat our mistakes.''

''Is that what you found in China?'' she asked quietly.

He hesitated. They had not spoken of his experiences there since that one, brief conversation. She had sensed his reluctance and had been unwilling to trespass on it. But now she could no longer resist. Something had made him the man he was, and she sensed that China held the key.

''I found...disappointment,'' he said slowly. ''I came away with a severely diminished sense of my own capabilities.''

He was silent, thinking, before he added, "I also found that I was no longer willing to settle for less than I really wanted. Life had simply become too precious."

"Poor Amanda," Petra said with a wry smile.

Giles smiled back. "One thing Amanda will never be is poor."

Perhaps not, but neither would she sit cross-legged before a table of wrought iron and glass, sipping fresh-made lemonade—made from actual lemons, no less—while a catbird sang in the nest beneath the porch eaves and a strong, sexy, tender man lounged nearby in companionable silence.

Not too bad. She tried to muster a flicker of homesickness for Manhattan but couldn't quite manage it. That set off a warning bell in her mind. Go easy, Petra, a little voice warned. This is all great but don't get carried away. Another couple of weeks and it's back to reality. Start betting on anything more and she'd be on a roller coaster ride in one direction only—straight down.

She flicked through several of the pictures. They were good, no doubt about that, but she couldn't muster much enthusiasm. Her new book, *Society*, would probably be as successful as the others she'd done—which meant considerably. But the topic that had held her attention for the past six months no longer seemed particularly important.

It was, like so much else of the work she'd done, glitzy in a dark, suggestive way, hinting at a great deal going on beneath the surface and enticing the viewer to become involved, to make his or her own decisions about what was happening. She took pride in being able to do that. But she couldn't help thinking that the pictures she'd taken of Dave and the others on the *Windstar* were somehow more important than these scenes culled from the Manhattan social whirl.

There was another one of Daryl talking to a tall, swarthy man whose face held a hint of danger, which had prompted the photograph. Most people in the scenes Petra had caught were self-consciously attractive, or trying to be. Daryl's friend—they looked as though they knew each other well—was anything but. He had a hard, pockmarked face suggestive of an upbringing very different from the privileged men and women around him. But he was also clearly wealthy, if the perfectly tailored tuxedo and the diamond pinky ring were anything to go by.

She frowned slightly, trying to put a name to the face. Nothing came to her. After a moment, she shrugged and went on.

The man did not appear in any of the other photos; he must have made only a brief appearance at the party she'd been shooting. But then lots of people did that, rushing from one party to another so they could rush to lunch the next day and regale their friends with how busy they were.

She flipped back through the photos until she found the one of the man and Daryl. Daryl looked like he always did, smoothly handsome, charming, complaisant.

She leaned a little closer. No, there was something else. An edge of nervousness around the eyes, almost deference. But that wasn't possible. Daryl wasn't deferential to anyone.

She looked at the man again. A beautiful woman hovered in the background. Petra knew her—Babushka something-or-other, or something like that. The latest hot model who had taken New York by storm, six feet plus of honey-blond hair and endless legs. Daryl's new friend who looked as though she was actually more interested in the other man. She was casting him the half-fascinated, half-terrified look a mongoose reserves for a snake.

Petra's frown deepened. Now, what made her think of that? Granted, the man looked tough, but that was no reason to equate him with a snake. What was it about him that made her think he was dangerous?

Slowly she held up the photo.

"What do you think of this one?"

Giles took it from her outstretched fingers. He glanced at it, looked again, and finally stared for several minutes. Quietly he said, "Who is he?"

"That's Daryl, you've seen other pictures of him."

"No, the man he's talking to."

"I don't know. Probably just someone who dropped by the party. Why, have you met him?"

Giles shook his head. "No, I'd remember." He glanced again at the man, frowning slightly, before handing the picture back to her.

"Are you going to use it?"

Petra hesitated. Strictly speaking, the picture wasn't in keeping with the tone of the book, but it compelled her attention all the same.

"Yes," she said, "I think I am."

"Smart. The blonde in the background has a particularly wolfish look people will remember."

Wolfish? Babushka—was that really her name?—wasn't faring too well with this one. First mongoose and now wolf. Yet Giles had a point, Petra thought as she looked more closely. The blonde did have a certain hungry edge to her, as though the man represented a huge, illicit treat she could hardly wait to gobble up.

Poor Daryl.

"Poor Daryl." She jumped slightly, startled to have spoken out loud.

"What's poor about him?" Giles demanded. He was feeling a whole lot better about the Daryl business since discovering that Petra had never slept with him. But he still didn't appreciate her feeling sympathetic toward the guy.

"I don't know," she admitted. "He's rich, attractive, in demand. I'm not sure why I always felt there was something missing from him."

"A brain?" Giles suggested dryly.

"No, he's smart enough. But he's one of those people who's always rushing here and there, always arranging things, as though he needs the activity to convince himself that he's real."

"Poor Daryl," Giles muttered. The guy was definitely getting on his nerves. It was time to change the subject.

He put down the note pad he'd been working on and stroked his fingers along the curve of Petra's bare arm. The tremor that raced through her brought a purely male light to his eyes.

"Don't you think we've been at this long enough?" he suggested.

"Ah...actually, I haven't gotten that much done."

"Neither have I. Let's take a break and start fresh."

"A break..." Petra murmured. She gazed down at his hand, lying dark and lean against her skin. Her mouth was suddenly dry. Unconsciously she touched the tip of her tongue to her lips.

"Yes," she said softly, "that sounds like a good idea."

An honest woman, her value is above pearls. The words of the old maxim turned over in Giles's mind as he stood up and crossed the small distance between them. His face was hard and intent, his eyes suddenly guarded. Deliberately he lifted her into his arms.

"You don't have to..." Petra began.

"I know," he said as he shouldered the door open and carried her inside. His step was swift and sure; his message was equally so. He had the strength and the will to claim her as his own.

Upstairs in the large, quiet room, he laid her gently on the bed, then stepped back a pace and began to remove his clothes matter-of-factly. Petra watched with frank fascination. He was a beautiful man, long of limb, lean and powerfully muscled, burnished by the sun, proud in his masculinity.

And gentle, infinitely, remarkably, devastatingly gentle. Brushing her hands aside, he undressed her himself. Each item of clothing was slowly and deliberately removed. When he unsnapped the front closure of her bra and lifted the lacy film away, his hooded eyes darkened. She caught her lower lip beneath her teeth as his fingers brushed over her nipples, bringing them to aching fullness. But when she tried to sit up, to move closer to him, his hands on her shoulders held her back.

"Wait," he said softly as he urged her back down onto the bed.

Mutely she obeyed. His hands slid down her narrow waist, lingering over the silken smoothness of her belly, to slip finally beneath the elastic of her underpants. He eased the fabric down her legs and tossed it aside, then came over her quickly, covering her with the warmth of his body.

"Now, Petra," he said huskily, his breath warm and moist against her throat. "Now for both of us."

Oh, God, yes, she thought dazedly as he began an exploration of her body and her senses that left her throbbing with need.

The most daring caresses made her gasp, but he soothed her with murmured words of admiration and delight that left her unwilling to deny him—or herself—anything. He was exquisitely tender, always controlled, until at the last that control shattered and he surged within her, her name on his lips, his hard body taking them both to incandescent pleasure.

Afterward, in the gray softness of recovery, Petra lay with her eyes opened, gazing up at the ceiling of elaborately carved wood. Giles lay beside her, his head against her breasts.

His hair beneath her fingers was damp and tangled. She could feel the racing pulse of his heart and the slick coolness of his skin. Slowly but inevitably, she was recovering her separateness from him, yet never so completly as it had been before.

It was that loss of self, that broaching of the clear barriers between her and all other people, that dismayed her. Since childhood, she had never known another way except to be separate and self-sufficient. Anything else was simply too dangerous.

Yet now she had opened herself to another, joined with him in the most intimate contact possible, and truly for a space of time forgotten where she stopped and he began.

No wonder people found love terrifying. The only part of life that brought an even greater loss of personal identity was death.

The mere thought of which startled her. She was not a morbid person. She and Giles had just shared an experience that was far more firmly rooted in life than in the end of it. Why then should she be thinking along such lines?

Giles raised his head. His hard features were relaxed, his dark brown eyes were slumberous. "Petra...?"

She smiled and touched a hand to his jaw darkened by a night's growth of whiskers.

"You looked miles away," he said.

"I was just thinking." She smiled. Inexperienced she might still be, but she wasn't insensitive. Not for anything would she tell him what had occurred to her.

Her smile deepened. "Thinking how incredible all this is...how incredible you are."

Giles was an unusually intelligent and caring individual with insights into people and a solid awareness of his own strengths and weaknesses. But he was also a man. One who had just made magnificent, unbridled love to a woman who stirred him as none other ever had. That being the case, he had no trouble believing her.

"You weren't so bad yourself," he murmured, the look in his eyes suggesting that she had been a good deal more.

His bronzed hand cupped her breast lazily as he smiled. "In fact, I'd say you have definite aptitude."

His breath caught slightly as he spoke. She'd worn him out, exploded him, turned him inside out, shattered every idea he'd ever had about women, sex... love. He was half convinced they'd stumbled onto some kind of hitherto-unsuspected universal force that was vaster and more powerful than anything ever known. He was trying to stay very calm, but his heart was still racing and he had a terrible, growing sense of his own vulnerability. He was in over his head, he was drowning. Trouble was, he didn't care.

"Is it... always like that?" Petra asked softly. Her cheeks were flushed. Her eyes were hidden beind the thick screen of her lashes. She looked absurdly, touchingly young and innocent. Worse yet, it was genuine.

"Uh... no," Giles said. He really had to remember how to breathe. There must be some trick to it. "No, it's not usually like that."

"Oh... I just wondered... how, uh, people could do it and then just go back to their ordinary lives, if that was how it was."

"No," he said again, "it's usually more . . . matter-of-fact. It feels good, you're glad you did it—or you're not—and it's over. That's all. This is . . . different."

Different, not better. His choice of words did not escape her. Maybe he didn't like having his soul left feeling as though it had been put through a food processor.

She cleared her throat. "Why do you think that is? That it was different, I mean. What causes that?"

Insanity, he almost said, but he stopped himself in time. She would take him seriously. Insanity wasn't the cause, although it might be the result. The cause was a whole lot more serious.

He raised his head and looked down at her gently. "I think it's because we're very lucky. Now, would you like a drink?"

He was evading her, she knew that. But it was all right. They were on the verge of something very dark and deep that she wasn't sure that she was ready to deal with. It might be better just to teeter on the edge of the cliff for a while.

Slowly, framing each word with care because reality still seemed very fragile, she said, "I would love a cup of tea."

## Chapter 9

She opted for iced tea served in tall tumblers filled with ice and decorated with sprigs of mint leaves. With it came a plate of tiny, buttery cookies served on a paper doily and ripe, scented peaches that burst in the mouth like celebrations of summer.

"I'm getting very spoiled," Petra said. She was sitting on the bed, wrapped in Giles's robe, which was miles too big for her. She'd rolled the sleeves up and tied the belt around herself twice, but she still felt engulfed in the scent and touch of him.

He'd put on a pair of shorts, and then only when she'd cast him a chiding glance. Stretched out on top of the sheets, listening to the old Victrola creak out reedy tunes of days gone by, he laughed.

"You're overdue for it."

A lifetime—almost—of crossword puzzles had left her with a tendency to relate one word to a host of concepts. Overdue reminded her that in the heat of their passion he had never failed to pause long enough to protect her. No child would result from her own careless innocence.

Would anything else?

Her cheeks were hot. She was tremulously afraid of being a fool.

"These are good," she said, forcing her attention on the tiny cookies that looked as though they had been made from elfin waffle irons.

"Somebody in the BIG recommended them," he said, shrugging. The BIG was the Block Island Grocery, almost the only place on the island to buy food and outrageously expensive. Even Petra, accustomed to Manhattan prices, had been shocked.

"Try one," she suggested, holding out the buttery confection.

He shook his head. "No, thanks. I don't much care for sweets."

Then why buy the cookies? The question was silent but understood all the same.

"I bought them yesterday." Thinking she might like them, wanting to please her, telling himself not to see how much of a fool he could be.

Women were very basic. His mother, his aunt, Amanda, every woman he'd ever known. His mother had wanted to be taken care of, to never have to strive on her own, to worry or fret. Young widowhood had not been part of the bargain. As soon as possible, she'd lost herself in frantic, mindless pleasure.

His aunt had wanted a child. She was one of those women who needed to invest herself in someone else before she could be complete. Thank heaven for them. He couldn't imagine what he'd have been without her. But still, there was nothing mysterious there, nothing complicated. Or maybe there was and he just hadn't ever wanted to think about it.

It was safer to think about Amanda. Beautiful, sensual, tantalizing, empty Amanda. Until Petra, he'd thought sex couldn't be any better. Now he'd discovered there was a vast other dimension to it that the Amandas of the world had never glimpsed.

A dimension where a man could very easily get lost forever.

"Have another cookie," he said.

She shook her head. "I'm full."

In fact, she wasn't, but a butter cookie couldn't fill the ache inside her. She remembered a time when she'd been six years old and in bed with chicken pox. At her mother's house, even though she was due at her father's. Her parents had spent hours on the phone discussing how to adjust visitation because she'd gotten sick and couldn't make the move when she was supposed to.

All she'd wanted were Oreos. To take apart, lick the center, eat each half separately. Not so much having cookies as engaging in some sort of methodical ritual that would take her out of herself and the mess she was in, just because she was six years old and couldn't tell them both to go to hell.

She was older now, all grown up and as free as anyone could get. Butter cookies wouldn't cut it.

"No," she said, looking at him. "I'm not full after all."

They changed the bed afterward, laughing as they pulled on the clean sheets to replace the old ones that had gotten stained with spilled ice tea and crumbled cookies.

Together they smoothed out the corners, fluffed the pillows, replaced the comforter. Giles bundled the used sheets and took them down to the laundry. When he returned, Petra was in the bathroom.

"I need to soak a while," she said, a little apologetically. She didn't want him to think for a moment that he'd hurt her; he hadn't. But she was new to this, after all, and they'd been very...enthusiastic. Hot water would feel good.

"All right," he said, frowning. He looked very big, standing here in the entrance to the bathroom with his arms crossed over his bare chest and the khaki shorts riding low on his hips.

He was going to watch her? She wasn't sure she could take that. She needed privacy, needed the freedom to retreat into herself, to rediscover herself.

He wasn't leaving. Indeed, if his stance was anything to go by, he knew perfectly well what she was thinking and wasn't about to give her the privacy she desired.

"Ah, Giles, could you...?"

It was his house. She couldn't exactly tell him to go. But she knew that he knew what she wanted, and she was starting to get annoyed now.

"I'm not used to an audience," she said.

He uncrossed his arms and took a step toward her. His face was suddenly pale underneath the bronzed tan. The determination she'd sensed had masked something far different.

"Are you going to run away again?"

She stared at him for a moment before she understood what he meant. There were a lot of different ways to escape, only some of which were physical. She could stay right here in his house, in his life, and still shut him out as effectively as if she'd disappeared.

He cared about that. He really and truly cared. It would hurt him if she closed herself off.

"No," she said quietly, looking him straight in the eyes. "I'm finished running."

He hesitated a moment longer before he nodded. "Okay." His expression lightened, making him look suddenly younger. "But don't stay in too long. You'll get pruney."

Alone in the bathroom, Petra stared down at the water. She had turned off the porcelain taps. The huge, claw-footed tub was full. Steam rose around her. Sunlight drifted in through the high windows. She could lie there by herself, letting her thoughts drift, alone and undisturbed.

Her hand was on the doorknob before she knew it. The bedroom was empty. For a moment, she almost panicked before she told herself not to be a fool, he was somewhere in the house or immediately outside.

He was in the kitchen, taking the blackberries they'd picked out of the refrigerator, but he started to put the container back when he saw her. "Something wrong?"

She stood in the high arched entranceway, wrapped in a white terry cloth towel that covered her to the thighs and no further. Her nipples ached, and she knew her face was flushed. But inside she felt absolutely calm.

"I just decided I'd rather not get pruney on my own," she said.

She'd overfilled the tub. Planning on one—and a slender one at that—she hadn't counted on the tidal effect of a large, muscular man.

"Oh, no," Petra exclaimed as she pulled herself out of the tub. Giles followed her. Together they spread towels on the floor to sop up the flow. Working fast, they bumped into each other. Their eyes met and they started to laugh.

"Want to try again?" Giles asked.

"Absolutely."

They were more careful this time, inching into the tub slowly until they were sure the water would stay in. It became a game, a little further, a little more, until they were both facing each other across the length of clear, shimmering heat.

"I like the beach now," Petra said, "but this is better."

"No sand," Giles said. He bestowed an engaging leer. "But doesn't this strike you as just a little strange?"

"Well, no, not actually. I mean, compared to a lot of other stuff I've heard about, it's pretty tame."

"Hmmm, we'll get back to that later. I was referring to the tub. The Victorians were the same size as we are or smaller, yet they built these immense tubs, far too large for just one person."

Petra's sapphire eyes widened. "Are you suggesting...?"

"There was more there than meets the eye."

"There isn't here," she said rather pointedly, looking down at the clear water.

Giles laughed. He particularly enjoyed her bouts of rueful shyness. They clashed pleasantly with the far more modern, independent side of her character. A side he didn't mind obliterating from time to time.

"Come here," he said softly.

Petra tilted her head to one side and looked at him. "Why should I?"

"Because I said so."

"Oh, caveman."

"No," he said matter-of-factly, "just man."

He had very capable hands, she thought a moment later. It was really remarkable how they could do exactly what he wanted without inflicting the smallest hurt. Certainly her ankles felt fine in their grip even as she was hauled across the tub and snug up against him.

"Not very subtle," she murmured. But highly effective. There might be some men who found hot water enervating; Giles wasn't one of them.

"Sex is like that," he said, his lips moving along her throat. "As subtle as a bolt of lightning or a summer storm that washes out everything in its path."

"Sex," Petra repeated slowly. Was that what happened between them? It seemed like such a cold, abrupt word to describe what was anything but.

But there was no time to think about it then, because Giles was doing devastating things with his mouth and hands. The last coherent thought she had was that he had to be right about the Victorians; their tubs were obviously designed for something besides bathing.

Afterward he said, "I'm afraid you didn't get to relax the way you wanted."

"It's all right," she said wryly. "I discovered there was something I needed more."

He froze in the midst of toweling her dry. His hands lingered along the curve of her hips. "What was that, Petra?"

"You, Giles. I needed you more than anything else." Ruefully she added, "I still do."

He straightened, looking at her from his great height. A lock of golden hair fell over his eyes. He brushed it aside impatiently. "Petra...we must talk...somehow we never get to do that, or at least not to talk about what's really important. What I think is on both our minds."

She nodded slowly. "What happens...after..."

After the ball, the old song said. In her case, it was after the vacation, when the time came to return to their own worlds. She to hers and he to his. What on earth were they to do?

"Talk," he repeated, his voice slightly strangled. They were standing very close together. The towel, forgotten, fell to the floor.

"We must," Petra agreed. But her eyes were on the broad, beautiful expanse of his chest—the same chest

## IT'S FUN! IT'S FREE!
## AND IT COULD MAKE YOU A
# MILLIONAIRE

If you've ever played scratch-off lottery tickets, you should be familiar with how our games work. On each of the first four tickets (numbered 1 to 4 in the upper right)—there are PINK METALLIC STRIPS to scratch off.

Using a coin, do just that—carefully scratch the PINK STRIPS to reveal how much each ticket could be worth if it is a winning ticket. Tickets could be worth from $5.00 to $1,000,000.00 in lifetime money.

Note, also, that each of your 4 tickets has a unique sweepstakes Lucky Number...and that's 4 chances for a **BIG WIN!**

## FREE BOOKS!

At the same time you play your tickets for big cash prizes, you are invited to play ticket #5 for the chance to get one or more free book(s) from Silhouette. We give away free book(s) to introduce readers to the benefits of the *Silhouette Reader Service™*.

Accepting the free book(s) places you under no obligation to buy anything! You may keep your free book(s) and return the accompanying statement marked "cancel." But if we don't hear from you, then every month we'll deliver 4 of the newest Silhouette Intimate Moments® novels right to your door. You'll pay the low members-only price of just $2.74* each—a savings of 21¢ apiece off the cover price—and there's no charge for shipping and handling!

Of course, you may play "THE BIG WIN" without requesting any free book(s) by scratching tickets #1 through #4 only. But remember, the first shipment of one or more book(s) is FREE!

## PLUS A FREE GIFT!

One more thing, when you accept the free book(s) on ticket #5 you are also entitled to play ticket #6 which is GOOD FOR A VALUABLE GIFT! Like the book(s) this gift is totally free and yours to keep as thanks for giving our Reader Service a try!

*So scratch off the PINK STRIPS on all your BIG WIN tickets and send for everything today! You've got nothing to lose and everything to gain!*

Here are your BIG WIN Game Tickets, worth from $5.00 to $1,000,000.00 each. Scratch off the PINK METALLIC STRIP on each of your sweepstakes tickets to see what you could win and mail your entry right away. (See official rules in back of book for details!)

*This could be your lucky day - GOOD LUCK!*

## TICKET 1
Scratch PINK METALLIC STRIP to reveal potential value of this ticket if it is a winning ticket. Return all game tickets intact.

LUCKY NUMBER

1J 988735

## TICKET 2
Scratch PINK METALLIC STRIP to reveal potential value of this ticket if it is a winning ticket. Return all game tickets intact.

LUCKY NUMBER

3R 990377

## TICKET 3
Scratch PINK METALLIC STRIP to reveal potential value of this ticket if it is a winning ticket. Return all game tickets intact.

LUCKY NUMBER

50 988500

## TICKET 4
Scratch PINK METALLIC STRIP to reveal potential value of this ticket if it is a winning ticket. Return all game tickets intact.

LUCKY NUMBER

9U 987883

## TICKET 5
We're giving away brand new books to selected individuals. Scratch PINK METALLIC STRIP for number of free books you will receive.

AUTHORIZATION CODE

130107-742

## TICKET 6
We have an outstanding added gift for you if you are accepting our free books. Scratch PINK METALLIC STRIP to reveal gift.

AUTHORIZATION CODE

130107-742

# YES! Enter my Lucky Numbers in THE BIG WIN
Sweepstakes and tell me if I've won any cash prize. IF PINK METALLIC STRIP is scratched off on ticket #5, I will also receive one or more FREE Silhouette Intimate Moments® novels along with the FREE GIFT on ticket #6, as explained on the opposite page. (U-SIL-IM 07/90) 240 CIS YAD7

NAME _____

ADDRESS _____ APT. _____

CITY _____ STATE _____ ZIP _____

Offer limited to one per household and not valid to current Silhouette Intimate Moments® subscribers.

©1990 HARLEQUIN ENTERPRISES LIMITED

PRINTED IN U S A

Carefully
detach card
along dotted
lines and
mail today!

Play
all your
BIG WIN
tickets
and get
everything
you're
entitled to—
including
FREE BOOKS
and a
FREE GIFT!

## BUSINESS REPLY MAIL

FIRST CLASS MAIL   PERMIT NO. 717   BUFFALO, NY

POSTAGE WILL BE PAID BY ADDRESSEE

SILHOUETTE READER SERVICE

## THE BIG WIN SWEEPSTAKES

901 FUHRMANN BLVD
PO BOX 1867
BUFFALO NY 14240-9952

she had kissed and licked her way across only a short time before—and she couldn't remember what talk was, let alone how to do it.

"Oh, no," he murmured thickly. "We're not doing this again, not yet. You need to rest."

Regrettably she realized that he was right. Petra offered no protest when he carried her to bed, nor when he laid her down on the cool, crisp sheets. When he joined her, she snuggled against him, warm and trusting in his arms.

They slept, heedless of the climbing sun or the busy world beyond them. Wrapped in their private idyll, they dreamed away the afternoon until the ringing door bell shattered their peace.

"I'm awfully sorry," Mrs. Kay said. "I wouldn't have bothered you, but I thought you'd want to know." She looked at the pair anxiously, clearly hoping that they wouldn't be offended by the island gossip that had made it clear where Petra could be found. "I did try to reach Ms. McNamara, but there was no answer at her apartment."

"You did the right thing," Petra said numbly. "I appreciate it." After a pause, she added, "Don't worry, I'll get through to Daphne."

And tell her what? That her lovely cottage, her hideaway from the real world that she had so kindly lent to her friend and client, had been burglarized? The real world had come to Block Island with a vengeance. Petra had only to look around at the shattered pane of glass, the upturned bookcases and the disheveled drawers to be sure of that.

"One of us should call the police," Mrs. Kay said tentatively. She was a short, slender woman in her forties who lived year-round on the island and was accustomed to the usual summer upheavals. This was something different, something far more serious.

"We'll contact them," Giles said quietly.

The older woman shook her head. "Kids, I suppose. Such a shame. We don't have this kind of thing here. Heavens, we don't even lock our doors."

Daphne had told Petra about that particular island habit, but it was one she couldn't bring herself to follow. She'd insisted on having a key and on locking the doors every time she went out.

It hadn't helped. Someone had jimmied the door, gone straight in and ransacked the house with devasting thoroughness. Not even the darkroom had been spared.

"We'll be all evening getting this cleaned up," Petra said faintly.

Giles's face was grim. "Then we'd better get to it."

"What about the police?"

"I'll call them now," he said. "You start making a list of whatever's missing."

Fifteen minutes later, Petra stood with her hands on her hips, looking around in bewilderment.

"I don't understand," she said. "If somebody goes to all the trouble of breaking into a house, shouldn't they steal something?"

"They usually do," the young, well-scrubbed police officer said. He scratched his head with one end of the pencil he'd had poised above his notebook. "Are you sure nothing's missing?"

"Not a thing," Petra said. "The television, microwave, clock radio, silverware, even the small computer Daphne keeps here are all exactly where I last saw them."

"How about cash?" the officer asked. "Does Ms. McNamara keep money here?"

Petra shook her head. The mere thought was amusing. Daphne kept her money in high-return securities. She considered any dollar left sitting around a wasted investment. Of all the people Petra knew, Daphne was the only one who didn't even keep leftover change.

"No," she said softly, "no money."

"Artwork?" he suggested, trying to be helpful. "She's an agent, right? She represents artists. Maybe she kept some of their work here."

Petra shook her head firmly. "She kept works in her gallery where they could be sold. A few are in her SoHo apartment, and there may be some in bank vaults. But here? Never."

"How can you be so sure?" the officer asked.

"Because Daphne represents mainly painters, and their work would be damaged by the high salt content of the air here. She might keep sculpture, but there was none when I arrived. As far as photographs go, they happen to be a hot market right now. Anything Daphne had, she had on display."

Convinced, the policeman jotted down a few notes, snapped the small book shut and shoved it into his back pocket. "Looks like that's about it."

"What are the chances of catching whoever did this?" Giles asked. He had been standing off to one side, observing the proceedings. His face was taut and grim.

The policeman glanced at him nervously. "Not real good, Professor Chastain. You know how fast folks can be out of here on the ferry."

"So you think it was day-trippers," Giles said. "Not locals?"

The policeman shook his head emphatically. "If we had locals doing this kind of thing, we'd know it."

"What about summer residents?" Giles persisted.

The policeman hesitated. Theoretically some attention should have been given to the people who rented houses on the island for a few weeks or months. But they were mainly families, often with small children, and they seemed intent on staying out of trouble. Or at least most of them did.

There was also another population of summer residents, mainly college students, who came to the island to work. The pay was good, but costs were high, too. And a lot of those kids knew that what they put aside would make the difference between finishing school and not.

"There's nothing special," the policeman said finally. "We've had the usual rash of drunk drivers, a few arrests for possession, and a mess of moped accidents. But nobody who might do this kind of thing."

"People on drugs steal for the money," Giles said.

"Yeah," the policeman agreed, "but nothing was stolen here, not even the stuff that could have been hocked pretty easily."

"Perhaps they were scared off," Petra suggested.

The young officer looked at her blankly. He'd been focused on Giles, answering his questions promptly and thoroughly. But Giles was known to him, he owned property on the island—significant property. And he was a man of reputation, a man known to the other men who worried about enforcing the law on the island. Petra, on the other hand, was an outsider.

"That's probably it," the younger man said. He looked again at Petra. "You were lucky."

She nodded, trying to make herself believe it. "Yes, or at least Ms. McNamara was. I'll have to call her."

She dreaded that. Daphne was her friend, but she had an undeniably excitable temperament. The knowledge that her house had been broken into would send her into a tizzy.

But Daphne surprised her. She listened to what Petra had to say without comment. For several moments afterward, she said nothing. Petra could hear only the static along the phone line. She had gotten to the point of thinking that they might have been disconnected when Daphne sighed deeply.

"It's time to come home, Petra."

Home? The word sounded strange. Petra had trouble realizing what she meant.

"Why?" she asked. "What's going on?"

"A crime wave apparently," Daphne said. Her voice, normally so strong and sardonic, trembled slightly. "I just got back from your studio. Somebody broke into it last night."

## Chapter 10

It was hot in New York. Also crowded, steamy, filthy and cacophonous. Petra's head pounded. Her lungs tightened in protest against the smog-filled air. One of the infamous temperature inversions was in effect, trapping pollutants so that they hung in sodden curtains of pink and yellow above the cityscape.

People hurried along, all of them seemingly intensely busy and preoccupied. Everyone had that blank stare carefully cultivated by the true New Yorker, the closest thing to personal invisibility. Everyone except a peddler with a blanketful of small, vividly painted canvases who sang out to them in the accent of the Caribbean.

"Come, pretty lady, come fine surh. I have good wares at fair prices. Come and look."

Smells twisted in the overheated air, the scents of hot dogs, sauerkraut and onions mingling with spicy souvlaki, shish kebabs and chili. People stood on the street corners eating their lunch or crowded into the restaurants found on every block.

Giles smiled wryly as he maneuvered the Land Rover through the congestion. "Restaurant...art gallery...restaurant...art gallery. Where do you go to buy food someone hasn't already prepared, or get a suit dry-cleaned, or find a hammer?"

"That's all here," Petra said, "you just have to look hard."

Giles glanced over at her. She looked very pale. The six-hour trip from Block Island had tired her. He could sense her frayed nerves and the tight control she was keeping on herself. Too tight. She'd have to let it go soon or risk even worse consequences.

"How long have you lived here?" he asked, seeking to divert her from thoughts of what they had to confront.

"Since I got out of college," she replied. "I was lucky enough to be able to buy a loft in one of the last of the old warehouses left for renovation. It was a wreck, but after all the work got done, it turned out well."

He wondered how she had been able to afford that when she was just beginning to establish herself. SoHo had become fashionable in the 1970s, sending real estate prices skyrocketing and forcing out many of the artists who had given the neighborhood its special character.

In their place had come an influx of yuppies in their pinstriped business suits and running shoes, anxious to live somewhere that made them feel as though they hadn't completely sold out. They still cared about art and culture; they were still just a little rebellious.

Certainly the rows of old stone and brick warehouses, many in the graceful style of the late 19th century, were a preferable alternative to the sterile boxes of the Upper East Side. Still, the popularity of SoHo had put the old buildings out of reach for most people—including most newly hatched college graduates interested in photography.

As though she had read his thoughts, Petra said, "My grandparents left me a trust fund that matured when I was twenty-one. Otherwise, I'd never have been able to do it."

"That was fortunate," he murmured, wondering if they'd done anything else to make up for the instability of her childhood. "Did you see much of them?" he asked.

She shook her head. "Hardly ever. I was stunned when it turned out that I was their principle heir." She smiled grimly. "My father still hasn't gotten over it. Neither has my mother, for that matter."

"Weren't they already divorced by then?"

"Most definitely, but my father figured the money should have been his, and my mother agreed, which meant, the way she saw things, that it should have been hers. The only thing they've ever seen eye-to-eye on is that I had no right to it."

She shrugged and brushed a strand of red-gold hair out of her eyes. "That's all water under the bridge. I love this place. It's still got a wonderful sense of vitality, and it's been perfect for my work.''

He could see how it would be. The neighborhood drew a variety of people, from the artists who were still hanging on, to the yuppies, to the tourists from Connecticut and New Jersey, all in search of enlightenment and maybe a bargain, although the first was elusive and the second nonexistent.

Above all, it was a place where people wore masks—of success, of talent, of taste—that in their own way revealed far more about the real individual than would otherwise have been possible.

That, he realized, was what she photographed—not fakery or pretense, but dreams. Often shallow and inconsequential dreams, but dreams nonetheless.

And she did it all with an unerring eye that managed to be both mercilessly acute and oddly gentle at the same time.

Which was all well and good if he wanted to dwell on the many and marvelous aspects of this woman to whom he was so intensely drawn. But whoever she was and whatever she did, she didn't deserve to have her life turned inside out by not one but two violations of her privacy.

Violations that no matter how hard he tried, he could not see as coincidence.

''There's Daphne,'' Petra said suddenly. She pointed out a tall, silver-haired woman whose razor-thin body was draped in bright purple jersey. Her strong, angular face was creased with a frown that lightened slightly when she saw Petra.

"There you are," she said. "I was getting worried."

Giles resisted mentioning that they had arrived almost to the minute of when they had said they would. The artist's representative was clearly worried, as she had every right to be.

"I'm so sorry about your house, Daphne," Petra said. "The good news is that there doesn't seem to be any real damage, just a mess."

"Forget it, honey," the older woman said. She put her arm through Petra's and looked at Giles pointedly. "There's a garage around the corner where you can park. We'll meet you upstairs, top floor. There's a deli in between here and the garage where you can pick up some food. All this stress is making me famished."

Giles resisted an urge to salute, smiled instead, and took himself off. When he was gone, Daphne grinned. "All that and nice, too. Darling, where did you find him?"

"We met on the island. I ran into him with a moped."

"Did you really? How clever of you."

"It was an accident."

"Haven't I always told you there's no such thing," Daphne reminded her as she led the way inside. The entry hall was small and musty with little more than a cluster of mailboxes, an intercom and a heavily locked door. Petra fished out her key and inserted it, noting as she did so that both door and lock appeared undamaged.

"The police think somebody let them in by accident," Daphne said. "Either that or they picked the lock, but it's a good one, so they'd have had to be professionals, which isn't likely."

"Why not?"

"Because they didn't take anything," Daphne said. "At least not so far as I can see. The stereo and TV are still there, along with your computer, the darkroom developer and enlarger, and your cameras. If they were pros, they would have been able to hock all that stuff for pretty good money."

Or they simply hadn't been interested in it to start with, Petra thought. She bit her lip as they stepped into the large industrial elevator that was a holdover from the building's warehousing days. It creaked and rattled its way up to the top floor, where it opened directly into Petra's loft.

When she had first seen the space, it had been a desert of peeling walls, warped floors, endless dust and no light. Even now she had to wonder where she'd found the nerve to buy it. But when the filthy windows and skylights had been scraped clean of a century of grime and sunlight flooded in, she'd begun to feel that she wasn't crazy after all.

Now stepping into the large, graceful expanse of bleached floors, lacquered walls, soaring pillars and hanging plants, she felt an oddly discordant sense. She was home, and yet she wasn't. It would have been very easy to attribute that sense of not-quite-right to the disorder, and Petra did try. But the effort rang hollow.

She was still mulling over why when Daphne said, "I thought it best to leave everything as it was. The police have been and gone. They told me fingerprints are for television detectives and the chances of catching anyone are practically nil. I got the impression that since nothing seems to be missing, they're not interested."

"I suppose they have better things to do," Petra murmured. In a city racked by drug-related crimes, that was an understatement. Still, through the haze of her numbness, she could feel the beginnings of anger.

How dare anyone do such a thing? Violate her privacy, touch her belongings, destroy the order and peace she had worked so hard to create? And do it with impunity, as though there were no laws, no protection, no justice.

She took a deep breath and reminded herself that she was actually lucky, particularly if Daphne was right and nothing had been taken.

A quick check confirmed that was the case. Petra's bewilderment deepened as she moved around the loft. The living area with its kilim rug, sand-hued couches and low glass tables was undisturbed, as was the dining area set off by pillars and occupied by a glass-pedestal table and eight bentwood chairs. Looking only at that part of the apartment, no one would guess anything had happened.

The rest was starkly different. Her work area seemed to have taken the worst of it. The darkroom appeared virtually disassembled, although all the equipment remained intact. The small office space with its white enamel work table, filing cabinets and single chair was a disaster. The furniture had been overturned, every drawer emptied and the contents strewn across the floor.

The bedroom and the kitchen were much the same. Every closet and cupboard had been emptied. Even the bookshelves were bare. Petra gasped as she looked more closely at the abandoned books. Many had been slashed.

"Maybe nothing's missing," she said bitterly, "because the thief was only interested in destroying."

Daphne took one of the books from her and frowned. She bent down to lift another...and another. "Look here. They're all cut in the same way. The front and end pages, the ones glued to the binding, have been cut open. Otherwise, they're undamaged."

The women stared at one another. Neither wanted to say what was obvious—whoever had broken into the loft had been searching for something they believed Petra might have gone to great lengths to hide.

"This didn't happen at the cottage," Petra said quickly.

"Maybe they didn't have time. People on the island keep a closer eye on their neighbors than anyone does here. They could have been scared off."

Petra took a deep breath. "It could have been a coincidence."

Daphne wrinkled her face. "Sweetie, there's a time to try to believe the best and there's a time to get real. You need to call the cops back and tell them what happened on the island."

"Good idea," Giles said as he stepped off the elevator. He was carrying a paper bag filled with groceries, which Daphne promptly took from him.

"Try to talk some sense into her," she instructed. "I'll fix us something to eat."

"I'm not hungry," Petra murmured.

"Don't be silly," Daphne said. "You'll eat something before you try to cope with this."

Her tone made it clear that there would be no further discussion. Stepping over a pile of pots and pans, she disappeared into the kitchen.

When they were alone, Giles looked around slowly. He stood with his hands in the pockets of his khaki trousers, his blond head tilted back, his face closed and expressionless.

Petra remained silent, watching him as he moved around the apartment, taking it all in for himself. Finally he said, "Do you have any idea what they were looking for, here and on the island?"

She shook her head. Her throat was suddenly tight, and she didn't trust herself to speak.

Giles cursed under his breath. He crossed the room in long strides and took her into his arms, holding her with gentle strength.

He did not speak, for which she was grateful. She couldn't have stood any false assurances. It was enough simply to lean against him, feeling the hard power of his body. For a few moments at least, she allowed herself the illusion of safety.

It disappeared when Daphne came back into the room carrying a tray with three glasses of wine, a plate of cheese and pâté, and a basket of crackers. She set the tray down on a table and looked at them both.

"So what are you going to do about this?"

She was speaking to Giles, not Petra. He seemed to see nothing unusual in that.

"Find out who did it," he said matter-of-factly.

"How?" Daphne asked. She was staring at him intently, her pale blue eyes hard and unrelenting. "The cops don't seem to have any idea."

Giles shrugged. "Of course not. Unless there had been a pattern of break-ins like this in the neighborhood, they'd have no way of knowing where to start."

"Maybe there has been," Petra said suddenly. "We should ask around, try to—"

"I already did," Giles said quietly. He sat down on one of the couches, prompting the two women to do the same. "Both the guy at the garage and the man who runs the deli say it's been very quiet. A few purse snatchings and a couple of drug busts, but otherwise, nothing."

He took a sip of his wine before he said, "If we can figure out what they—or he or she, whichever it was—were looking for, then we'll have a shot at figuring out who did this."

"There has to be more than one person involved," Petra said quietly. "There were two break-ins more than a hundred miles apart."

Giles shook his head. "They didn't necessarily happen at the same time just because that's how we found out about them. Remember, you hadn't been spending much time at the cottage."

Daphne raised her eyebrows but didn't comment. "He's right, sweetie. One person could have done both. So the question is: who have you really annoyed lately?"

"I don't know," Petra replied. She managed a faint, dry laugh. "There are so many."

Giles turned to Daphne. "Is that true?"

The agent sighed. "Petra's work is controversial, that's why it sells. She has a tendency to see more than some people like."

"But she's still welcomed everywhere—no one you know of tries to avoid her?"

"Maybe some do," Daphne said, "but not so as you'd notice. She's hot, she's now, she's in demand. People she photographs get noticed, and most people around here are desperate for that. Even an unattractive photograph by Petra O'Toole is better than none at all."

Giles glanced around at the ransacked loft. "Somebody doesn't agree."

"No," Daphne said grimly, "somebody doesn't." She hesitated a moment before she asked, "Is it possible this is less professional than personal? There wouldn't have been any embarrassing little mementos lying around, the kind that seemed like a good idea at the time but not later?"

A warm flush darkened Petra's cheeks. "No," she said quietly, "there wouldn't have been."

"Well, then, I absolutely don't know what to make of this." Daphne helped herself to a slice of pâté while she thought it over.

"Oh, well," she said finally, "I suppose we'll never know."

"Why not?" Petra sked.

"Because they must have gotten whatever they were looking for," Daphne said, pointing out what she thought must have been obvious. "You had work here and at the cottage. Both places were ransacked. Face it, honey, whatever they wanted is gone."

Petra was about to reply when she caught a warning glance from Giles. She took a sip of her wine instead and listened as he deftly turned the conversation in other directions. He and Daphne chatted about Block Island. Although the agent spent relatively little time there, they knew some of the same people and had the same views about how the island needed to be protected.

Petra's eyes were beginning to feel heavy. Several times she lost the thread of the conversation. Finally, when she thought she couldn't hold sleep off a moment longer, she looked up to find that Daphne was gone.

"What happened?" she murmured groggily.

Giles knelt in front of her. "You drifted off." He touched her face gently. "Are you all right?"

"Fine...just tired..." She struggled to sit up, only to find that she didn't have to. Giles was lifting her into his arms.

"You keep doing this," she said, the words sounding very faint and far away. "It's getting to be a habit."

He smiled but otherwise didn't reply. He laid her down in the bedroom, removed her shoes and covered her with a thin blanket.

On the brink of sleep, Petra was without her usual defenses. Days—and nights—of Giles's company had underminded her stalwart self-reliance. Instinctively she grasped his hand.

"Don't go," she whispered in the instant before unconsciousness claimed her. Before she could see the grim look that crossed his face at the realization that she still thought him capable of leaving her.

## Chapter 11

The warm, firm grip of Giles's hand came back to haunt Petra the next morning. She stared at herself in the bathroom mirror, trying to reconcile the strong, capable woman she knew herself to be with the tremulous, fearful creature she had turned into the night before.

It was so easy. Giles invited her in every possible way to depend on him. He would need very little encouragement to take over entirely. And she probably needed even less to let him.

Wearily she shook her head. Though she had slept dreamlessly, she still felt tired. Her eyes were darker than usual, closer to gray-blue than sapphire. Her hair looked limp, although she had to admit that a few swats with a brush would restore it. But first a shower.

She stood for a long time under the warm pulsing water, letting it blank out her thoughts. By the time she emerged, wrapped in a terry cloth robe, she could smell the aromas of coffee and bacon coming from the kitchen.

She dried her hair quickly, put on enough makeup to look at least semirested, and slipped into lavender slacks and a mauve T-shirt. The combination was ordinarily one of her favorites, but that morning it made her wince.

Petra had to pass through the bedroom to reach the kitchen. Earlier when she'd awakened, she hadn't been thinking very clearly. But now she couldn't help but see that much of the mess from the previous day had been picked up. Clothes were back in the closet or stacked neatly on the dresser waiting for her to put them in the right drawers. Books were back on their shelves. Little was left to indicate there had ever been an intruder.

It was the same in the kitchen. Giles stood at the stove, his sleeves rolled up, looking perfectly at home as he beat eggs in a metal bowl and kept an eye on the bacon he was frying.

He smiled when he saw her. "Morning. Feeling hungry?"

She made a noncommittal sound, only to have her stomach provide its own response. The growl was loud enough to startle them both.

Giles laughed. "I guess so. Sit down, I'll get you some coffee."

"I'll do it," Petra murmured. She poured herself a cup and glanced at him out of the corner of her eye.

He looked too darn good, never mind that he was unshaven and his clothes were wrinkled. He was still the most stunningly attractive man she had ever encountered. She had only to close her eyes to see, unbidden, the image of him naked and hard, drawing her with him into a vortex of passion where she could so easily forget her own existence.

Her eyes jerked open. Giles was looking at her expectantly.

"What was that?" she asked.

"How do you like your eggs?" he repeated patiently.

"Actually I'm not big on breakfast."

"You didn't eat anything last night," he pointed out. "You need something in your stomach."

He was right, of course. Reluctantly she said, "Scrambled, please, and dry. I'll fix some toast."

They worked side by side in silence for several minutes until the food was ready. When they were seated at the table, Petra took a forkful of the eggs. Her eyes widened in surprise.

"These are good."

He laughed. "Anything would taste good to you right now, but they aren't bad. I added a little grated Swiss cheese and a few chives. Perks them up."

The toast, on the other hand, was burned. Giles graciously claimed he liked it that way. His tolerance rankled.

"I noticed you straightened up quite a bit," Petra said.

"I didn't think you should wake up to the same mess. I tried to put things where I thought they went, but I may have made some mistakes."

"That's all right," she murmured. He was being so damned nice. Kind, thoughtful, considerate, modest. Next to him she felt like a total ingrate. It was more than she could stand.

"I really appreciate everything you've done," she began.

He put down his fork and looked at her. "I haven't done anything, Petra."

"Of course you have. You came all the way here with me when you certainly didn't have to, you stayed last night when I have to admit I was a little nervous, and you helped clean up. What more could you possibly do?"

"Find whoever did this," he said and picked up his fork again.

She laughed nervously. He really wasn't going to take the hint. "I have a theory about that. I think it was just someone I annoyed, like Daphne said, and now that they've done this, they'll be satisfied. We'll never hear from them again."

"That's a hell of a supposition."

"It makes sense," she contended. "My work is controversial, it stands to reason someone could have gotten annoyed."

"And you don't think they could still be that way?"

Petra shrugged. "I don't see why they should be. They must have gotten whatever they wanted."

"Really?" He looked at her across the table, his eyes gleaming with the amber light she had already come to associate with danger. "What about the photos at my house? They're undisturbed. No one except you and me even knows where they are."

"That's true," she murmured, silently damning the relentless intelligence that had made him recognize what she herself was still trying to deny. "But they're only a tiny part of my work. The odds that they would be of interest to whoever did the break-ins are—"

"Overwhelming," he interrupted. "Two break-ins so close together with identical search patterns indicate someone is looking for something in particular. Moreover, something that you could have been expected to have with you on Block Island. That means recent work, the photos for your next book, not anything else."

"All right, maybe it does. Which is an excellent reason for getting those pictures out of your house as quickly as possible. I'm sure you don't want to be involved any more than you already are."

He shot her a hard, quelling look. "What makes you think that?"

She laughed nervously. "It's obvious, isn't it? No one wants to buy into somebody else's problems."

"If our positions were reversed, would you walk out on me?"

"Of course not, but nobody's talking about walking out. You just need to get on with your life and I need to get on with mine." Her voice cracked slightly, but she ignored it and plunged on. "That's all this is about."

It wasn't, but Giles understood this wasn't the time to force that particular issue. She was running scared—of him, of herself, of whoever was behind the break-ins. That last part had shattered any illusion she'd had about physical safety, and her emotional equilibrium had been disrupted as well. He was rock-certain of that because exactly the same thing had happened to him. He knew the symptoms.

"As it happens," he said quietly, "I'd like to spend a few days in New York."

At her skeptical look, he went on, "I've been offered a job at Columbia University. I need to follow up on that, think about whether or not it's what I want to do. And I need to touch base with my publisher."

All of which was hooey. The job at Columbia was real enough, but he'd already talked with the people involved and had all the information he needed. As for the publisher, he and Giles had managed to conduct a highly pleasant and mutually profitable relationship through six years of phone calls and letters. Closer contact, while enjoyable, was hardly necessary.

"That's great," she said, her eyes suddenly alight. "About Columbia, I mean. Do you really think you might take the job?"

Giles hesitated. His first response had been thanks, but no thanks. Now he wasn't so sure. Life on the island, while it had many attractions, was a bit too isolated for his taste. A year ago, he wouldn't have thought that possible.

He'd rebounded from the wounds of China straight into a relationship with Amanda that had left its own legacy of cynicism and world-weariness. He'd wanted nothing so much as to withdraw to someplace where he couldn't be hurt or disappointed any further.

But he realized now how unrealistic that had been and how ultimately unsatisfying. He had Petra to thank for revitalizing him. He was going to repay the favor whether she liked it or not.

"That's what I have to decide," he said finally. "But in the meantime, I'll be staying around for a while."

Petra could not hide her relief, although she tried. "That's fine then," she said. "If anything more happens with this, I'll let you know."

"That won't be necessary."

"Oh, but I thought—"

"It won't be, because I'll be right here with you, and if anything does happen, I'll be the second—if not the first—to know."

"Here...you mean you want to stay—"

"Right here, in your apartment, with you." He smiled faintly. "Do you have any objection to that?"

Petra shook her head dazedly. "No, I guess not...I mean considering our relationship...that is, the kind of relationship we've been having...it makes sense, I suppose, for you..."

"Good," he said, making a mental note not to keep on with this tendency to interrupt her. Right now, when she was fumbling around like mad trying to work her way out of a situation that made her so insecure, he could excuse himself for interjecting a little assistance. But when circumstances got back to normal, she wouldn't like it. Besides, it wasn't polite, and he was, at rock bottom, a courteous man. At least most of the time.

Petra frowned. There was obviously an etiquette to this sort of thing. What exactly did one do when a lover moved in a for a few days? Make him feel at home, she supposed, exactly as Giles had done for her.

"I'll clear up," she offered when they had finished breakfast. "After all, you cooked."

"Fine," Giles said. "If you don't mind, I have a couple of calls to make."

She suggested that he use the phone in the bedroom where he would have some privacy. She presumed he'd be talking to the people at Columbia, and Giles said nothing to discourage her.

But once in the bedroom, he used his credit-card number to place a call to Block Island. The chief of police was a hard-headed islander with too much experience to be surprised by anything. He readily agreed to put a guard on Giles's house during his absence. If anyone came sniffing around, they'd get more than they bargained for.

He also agreed to remove certain items from the house and express-mail them to Giles in New York.

"Ought to make the afternoon ferry okay," he said. "With a little luck, you'll get them tomorrow."

The two men talked awhile longer before Giles hung up. By the time he had returned to the kitchen, Petra had finished clearing away the dishes. She was standing in front of the open refrigerator, frowning.

"There's not much in here," she said. They'd almost exhausted the supplies Giles had picked up the day before. The cupboard—so to speak—was embarrassingly bare.

"Let's go shopping," she suggested, "and while we're at it, I'll give you the quarter tour."

She did better than that. For the remainder of the day, they tromped through every nook and cranny of the neighborhood south of Houston Street—hence its name, SoHo. The graceful cast-iron buildings intrigued Giles. Built as warehouses and factories, many nonetheless had been designed to resemble Venetian palaces, Second Empire mansions, and the like. They evoked a vanished era, when even the most mundane tasks were surrounded by an aura of excitement and purpose.

Not that there was anything mundane about the neighborhood now. Despite its recent transformation into a fashionable district, some of the buildings were still used for manufacturing. Trucks further clogged the already congested streets, stalling traffic and causing pedestrians to pick their way through gingerly.

The slow-going didn't seem to bother anyone, not when there were such ample distractions. Giles's eye was caught by a gallery displaying works of African tribal art. An immense wooden idol with cut-stone eyes stared back at him. Next door was a display of glasswork so finely wrought that the pieces looked like gossamer. Immediately next to it was a shop selling antique clothes. He did a double take at the vision of an upper-class Victorian lady who seemed to be standing directly inside the door.

"What on earth . . . ?" he began. The vision turned out to be a mannequin, but the effect was uncanny all the same. He had the sudden sense of having seen at last one of the people he had spent so many years studying about.

"Would you mind if we went in here for a moment?" he asked Petra.

She shook her head. The shop was cool and dark after the heat outside. It was relatively new in the neighborhood. Petra had yet to visit it. She stood, looking around bemusedly, as Giles moved purposefully about.

If Great-aunt Emmeline had possessed a cluttered attic, this would have been it. Trunks and bandboxes abounded. From them spilled clothing of all description, some ragged and worn, some surprisingly fresh and crisp despite their years.

Tentatively Petra picked up a delicate piece of lace and held it to the light. "I can't imagine anyone taking the time to make something like this, lovely as it is."

Looking through a stack of books piled up on an old rolltop desk, Giles said, "It's machine-made."

"What? You mean it isn't genuine?"

"Not at all. I'd guess it dates from the 1890s, maybe slightly earlier. Lace was a very popular item. It was made in enormous quantities. That's why there's still so much of it around."

"Oh," Petra said, feeling faintly disappointed. She set the lacy square back down. "I thought the Victorians made everything by hand."

Giles shot her a startled look. "You did?"

"I never said I knew much about history," she murmured defensively. "I just thought...it was a simpler time, people weren't as distracted as now, there was no television.''

"So they sat around making lace?" He smiled gently. "'Fraid not. If they sat around doing anything, it was dreaming up new machines to make lace—and everything else—for them. Their world had an insatiable appetite for goods. The only way it could be fed was to take production out of the cottages and into the factories.''

"What a shame," Petra murmured. "I guess they had no idea what they were doing.''

"On the contrary," Giles said quietly, "they knew exactly. Most of them were hoping to make life better for everyone. They had what in retrospect seems like a naive belief in the benefits of machinery, but their objectives were good.''

He leaned over to an open armoire and picked up a pair of high-buttoned shoes. The leather was dull and cracked across the instep, but it was still possible to imagine a woman putting those shoes on, going out to stroll through the world of 1880 or 1890.

"Look at these," Giles said. "They're well-made, sturdy and probably comfortable. They could have belonged to a middle-class woman, the wife of a teacher, say, or a small businessman. But they could also have belonged to a shop girl or a factory worker who earned them for herself. And that's what makes them important. Up until that time, there was a tremendous gap between the haves and the have-nots. You could tell what social class a person belonged to just by looking at him or her. After the Victorians came along, it wasn't so easy. Social classes blurred, opportunities broadened, people became more equal. We're still benefiting from that today."

"All because of a pair of shoes," Petra murmured. She wasn't really being flippant; what he was saying had gotten through to her. Everybody longed for a simpler world, but no one wanted to pay the cost of it.

Giles was right. People nowadays could mingle far more freely than ever before. With the right clothes—and that was very open to interpretation—almost anyone could go anywhere. She'd been to parties where it was impossible to tell who had actually been invited and who had crashed, who had money and who didn't, who was on the level and who wasn't, who—

"Giles," she said suddenly. Her face had gone very pale. The hand she reached out to him trembled slightly.

He was at her side instantly. Gently he slipped an arm around her waist, taking her weight against his own. "What is it?"

"Those photographs, the ones I left at your house, I need to see them again."

He gave her a long, level look before he said, "Yes, I know. They're on their way. We should have them by tomorrow."

"How did you know I'd want to...?"

"It has to be somebody in those photos, Petra," he said gently.

"Somebody who doesn't belong," she murmured, thinking of the clothes again, the disguises and the masks, the pretenses and the poses. All those people pretending to be something they weren't just to be something at all.

Thinking, too, of how he had known before she'd been willing to admit the truth to herself. No random violence, no halfhearted harassment, but something real, dangerous, immediate. And continuing.

"Or who belongs too well," Giles murmured under his breath.

She didn't understand his meaning, but she was too distracted to pursue it. Slowly she turned away from the jumbled displays of the past, into the bright light of the unrelenting present.

"Come on," she said, still holding his hand, "we've got shopping to do."

## Chapter 12

They went to Paglacci's for sweet, honey-cured ham, pepper salami and crispy miniloaves of bread. At a corner fruit market, they bought avocados, radicchio and tender bibb lettuce. Down the street, in a shadowy warren beneath a green-and-yellow awning, they found good Chianti—the kind *without* the straw basket—and very old cognac, so aged that it would have to be decanted with the greatest care. They carried everything home in string bags and covered the counters of Petra's sterile kitchen with happy abandon.

While Giles took care of the food, she wandered out into the living area of the loft. David Bowie was on the stereo. She took him off and put on Vivaldi instead. The low glass table was set with turned-wood candlesticks she had picked up in Milan. From a hidden closet, she unearthed inlaid tile trays that served as place mats. When she was done, she cranked louvered shades down over the skylights and the floor-to-ceiling windows, filling the loft with gently shaded light.

They ate seated cross-legged on the kilim, listening to the Vivaldi and feeding each other tastes between sips of the crisp, slightly cool wine.

As though by mutual accord, they did not talk about the break-ins or the photographs. Giles asked her questions about her work—how she had gotten started, when she'd first realized she had real ability, what had brought her to New York.

"I was always taking pictures," Petra said in between bites of avocado. "I can't remember a time when I didn't have at least one camera strung around my neck. When I was eight, I used my allowance to buy some developer and tried to improvise a darkroom." She smiled at the memory. "It was a disaster."

"What happened?" Giles asked.

"I had no infrared light, so I had to work completely in the dark. I ended up knocking the developer over, destroying the bathroom counter and almost asphyxiating myself in the process. If anyone had struck a match at that moment, the whole house would have gone up."

"Whose house? Your mother's or your father's?"

"My father's," she said quietly. "He wasn't at home, and I tried to clean up the damage before he arrived, but that really wasn't possible."

"What did he do?" Giles asked.

"Nothing. I really expected to be punished, but he didn't seem to care. He'd just broken up with his latest girlfriend, and I guess that had him preoccupied. All he wanted to do was talk about how rotten life was and how nothing ever worked out the way it was supposed to."

"He said all this to you?" Giles asked, refilling their wineglasses. The candles flickered gently. They weren't really necessary, it wasn't dark yet, but they lent an air of darting possibility to the scene.

"He told me everything," Petra said with a shrug. "I was his sounding board as well as my mother's. Every move they made, every relationship they had, every disappointment they suffered, I heard about."

"But when you brought dangerous chemicals into the house and almost blew yourself up, you didn't hear a word."

Petra shrugged. She was embarrassed about having told him so much. Her past was something she rarely discussed.

"It's not a big deal," she said. "Maybe they did me a favor. After all, I never had to get over a lot of illusions."

"About what?"

"People, men and women, relationships. I've always understood that everything is temporary, nothing lasts. The trick is to keep from getting hurt."

He resisted the impulse to tell her that if she was trying to provoke him with this modern nonsense about nothing being permanent, she was succeeding. Instead, he said, "Is that why you take pictures, to try to capture some of those very temporary moments?"

It was a serious question, intended to provoke a serious answer. Petra, however, laughed.

"How would I know? I take pictures because it's the only thing I can do. It's fun, it's satisfying, and it pays great. What could beat that?"

"Nothing I can think of," Giles murmured dryly. There she went, sliding away again, hiding behind flippancy like a little girl darting behind a tree. He could still see her, peering out at him, wary of what he would say and do. The need to reassure her far outweighed the desire to confront the reasons for her evasiveness.

"The music is beautiful," he said quietly. "But let's put on something we can dance to."

He chose the unabashedly romantic melodies of Strauss, then teased her for having them in the first place.

"I have all sorts of stuff," she murmured as he drew her up from the table. In his arms, feeling the strength of him against her, she had to admit that the music made more sense than it ever had to her before.

She'd bought it as a joke, because Daphne accused her of knowing nothing about anything that had happened more than twenty minutes before. The Strauss, the Vivaldi, even a few Elizabethan chants, were her secret concession to a different world. A world that lasted.

A world where it seemed natural for a man and woman to dance together touching, for the man to take the lead, for the woman to be unperturbed by that because it didn't threaten her in any way. It even felt right for the soft cotton hem of her skirt to brush lightly against her bare legs, for her hair to fall over her shoulders and over the hand against her back, for her perfume to rise on the warm afternoon air, tantalizing them both.

They danced in a silence of words that rang with unspoken truths. And when the music finally stopped, they remained close together, bodies touching, the world forgotten.

His mouth was warm and hard, his body enticing. Petra let her head drop back as her eyes fluttered closed. He'd been right about the photographs, about the need to capture and keep the tiny slivers of quicksilver time. This was another part of the Giles scrapbook she was mentally keeping. The pages of it were drifting by so quickly. Sure they would run out soon.

But first...there was the long afternoon fading into evening, the distant sounds of the city beyond the windows and the intimate closeness of their bodies twining on the huge bed amid the smooth white sheets and the jumbled pillows; soft pale skin and bronzed hardness, male and female.

Much later, she stirred, satiated and drowsy with love, to see Giles standing by the bed. It was dark now and the lights were off. Only a single flame showed, the candle he had lit.

He set the candle on the table near the wall. Slowly, his strong hands moving carefully, he decanted the old cognac, keeping the amber liquid before the flame to make sure that no impurities slipped from it.

Naked, he came across the room and handed her one of the snifters. He said nothing, merely smiled, as she touched her lips to the fiery sweetness.

The same taste was on him when he joined her, teasing the corners of her mouth with his tongue.

"Like it?" he murmured.

Dazed, uncertain exactly what he meant, she nodded.

"It's very old," he reminded her. "In fact, it's been around almost forever."

"Some things," she said before speech deserted her, "get better over time."

His smile deepened as he lowered his head. Thick, golden hair brushed her nipples. She felt the velvet roughness of unshaven cheeks against their aching fullness.

"I count that as a victory," Giles said huskily in the moment before he drew her back down with him onto cool, rumpled sheets and into hot, throbbing pleasure.

She awoke to a stridently ringing bell and automatically lashed out a hand for the telephone, only to discover that it wasn't the culprit. The bell went on for a long moment after she lifted the receiver, only to be abruptly cut off.

Petra sat up slowly. She felt only half awake, uncertain of the time or of what was happening. Swinging her feet to the floor, she reached for the sheet to cover herself.

At the bedroom door, she could hear voices, but they were gone by the time she came out into the main part of the loft. Giles was standing near the kitchen, wearing the slacks and shirt he had pulled on hastily. He had an express mail package in his hand.

"They're here," he said quietly. "I'll fix some coffee, then we can go over them."

She wanted to say that she'd fix the coffee, it was her kitchen after all, and that she didn't need his help going over her photographs.

But she was always bitchy in the morning, and she'd learned long ago how to deal with it. It was some kind of chemical thing that could be defused only by a hot shower and plenty of caffeine. She was also far too grateful to anyone who would make her a cup of coffee to complain about kitchen rights.

She emerged, her hair wrapped in a towel and her body swathed in a terry cloth robe that had definitely seen better days. Taking the steamy mug he offered, she perched on one of the kitchen stools.

He had already opened the envelope and spread out its contents on the counter. Slowly they went through them together.

"Who's the guy with Cissy what's-her-name?" Giles asked.

Petra peered more closely at the photo. Behind the blond Cissy with her leveraged buy-out smile was a young, callow man in a shirt the collar of which looked too big for him. He had a drink in one hand and a cigarette in the other. The direction of his gaze made it clear he was staring straight down Cissy's ample cleavage.

"That's Bobby Harkness," Petra said. "I don't think we need to worry about him."

"Why not?"

"He's thirteen years old."

Giles's eyes widened. Petra felt a spurt of unreasoning pleasure at the knowledge that she had finally managed to knock him off balance. But it was short-lived, as she realized that his obvious shock was well placed. Bobby Harkness was a tragedy waiting to happen.

"You're not serious," Giles said. "He can't be thirteen."

"He's big for his age," Petra acknowledged. "He's one of the Harknesses, old money and plenty of it. I have no idea where his parents are or why they let him do what he does, but I do know that Bobby's been on the social circuit for at least two years. He turns up at a lot of the 'in' parties. He's not the only one, either. There are at least half-a-dozen girls in his age group and probably as many boys who show up regularly."

"Why aren't they just sent home to bed?" Giles demanded caustically.

Petra hesitated. She had trusted Giles with her innocence and had no regrets. But she was beginning to realize that he had a kind of innocence of his own, different from hers and in some ways far more vulnerable.

Slowly she said, "Sometimes they are, but not alone. Kids like Bobby are very appealing to jaded tastes. Particularly since it's possible to pretend that there's really nothing wrong with giving them what they so obviously want."

"You can't believe that," Giles insisted.

"Of course I don't. Kids like Bobby are on a one-way street to self-destruction. It's the same whether they're poor and in the ghetto or rich and at the best parties. They still end up burned out and used up."

"And nobody cares?"

Petra took a long sip of her coffee before she said, "I care. I tried to talk to Bobby and a couple of the others awhile back. I won't repeat what they said because it was particularly foul, but the gist of it was that I should mind my own business. They don't see anything in life except looking good and having fun, so they go for it as fast as they can."

"Are you going to use this picture?" Giles asked, fingering it with a distaste.

Petra nodded. "It's a good one, it will make people think. And maybe—just maybe—somebody who knows Bobby will recognize him and try to do something."

Giles took a deep breath and let it go slowly before he nodded. "All right, let's go on. What about this one?"

Slowly, methodically, they went through the pile of prints. To most of the faces, Petra could put a name. But a few stumped her.

"That's not really surprising," she said. "Lots of people crash these parties, some of them once or twice, others as a regular habit."

"But they don't attract much attention," Giles replied.

"I suppose not," she agreed.

"What about this guy?" He pointed to the picture of the hard-faced man talking with Daryl.

Petra hesitated. The face continued to disturb her. "I was thinking about him," she said quietly, "yesterday when we were in the clothing store. You were talking about how clothes used to really set people apart and now they don't. It occurred to me that even though he's dressed right, he doesn't seem to fit in.''

"Yet he's accepted. Daryl looks excited just to be talking to him and the tall blonde . . . probably the less said about her, the better.''

"We could be reading too much into this," Petra cautioned. "It's just one photo.''

"Shouldn't he be in some of the others, at least in the background?''

"Yes," she acknowledged, "he should be. It looks as though he didn't stay at the party very long. Just made an appearance and left.''

"And you have no idea who he is?''

She shook her head. "None, but so what? Just because he looks different . . .''

"I want to run this by a friend of mine," Giles said quietly. "Do you have a fax machine?''

Petra nodded slowly. "Yes, but I don't really think this is necessary.''

"Humor me." He took the photo from her and went over to the small work area. Much of it had been straightened up, but the fax machine remained buried under piles of folders thick with old photos.

"I don't use it very often," Petra explained as she unearthed the machine. "Daphne gave it to me because she said I wasn't eating right.''

Giles stared at her thoughtfully. "No, don't tell me, let's see if I can work that out. You weren't eating right because you don't like to cook. Lots of take-out restaurants have faxes now. You can fax them an order, and it will be waiting when you get there. Daphne figures you'd go for that."

"That's very good," Petra said admiringly. "It took me a week to figure out what I was supposed to use it for."

"And did you?" he asked, laughing.

"Once. I faxed an order, then got busy working and forgot to pick it up. Now, if they could fax me the food, that would be a different matter."

"Somehow," Giles said, "I am going to convince you of the pleasures of cooking food, eating food and—" he leaned closer seductively, his voice dropping to a husky whisper "—cleaning up afterward."

Petra feigned a delicious shiver. "Oh, I don't know if I could go that far, Professor Chastain. Cleaning up with a man? That sounds pretty risqué."

"It worked out okay in our big tub," he reminded her.

Our. The word hung in the air between them. He'd used it inadvertently, but the significance didn't escape him, or her. He was beginning to think of them as a couple.

For Petra, dyed-in-the-wool individualist and loner, that was a proposition she wasn't ready to confront.

"About the fax," she murmured, looking away from him.

He nodded and let her go. Moments later, a copy of the photo was on its way to Paul Delacroix in Washington.

* * *

"What would you like to do today?" Petra asked a short time later as they were having breakfast at a nearby cafe.

He tore a flaky croissant apart and spooned marmalade from a stoneware crock. "Go to a party."

"You're kidding, a party?" He might as well have said that he wanted to climb in the monkey cage at the zoo. Parties—especially the kind she went to—just didn't seem like something he'd want to do. "Are you sure?"

"Why not? Isn't that what people do around here?"

"Yes, but...it's still summer...there aren't very many people in town."

"It's a weekday," he reminded her. "Something must be going on."

She glanced at him over the rim of her coffee cup. He looked perfectly pleasant, devastatingly handsome as usual, and involved in his croissant. He was also giving off waves of implacable determination that made it clear he wasn't going to take no for an answer.

"I suppose I could call Daphne," she said doubtfully.

"Good idea."

"But I really doubt there'll be anything worthwhile," she added hastily.

He flashed her a quick, relentless smile. "Let's find out."

What was it about New York? Petra wondered. Just when it seemed to have straightened itself out, imposed some sort of order and routine, even settled on a schedule, everything went to hell in a hand basket.

It was the end of August, for heaven's sake. The dog days, the doldrums, the absolute nadir of the social season. No one, but no one, was supposed to be in town. Okay, maybe seven million people or so were milling around, but they weren't the party crowd. All of them were out in the Hamptons working on their tans, or hiking in Nepal or purifying themselves at ashram/health clinics in New Mexico. They were not braving the dirt and grime of New York in the summer in order to have parties.

Except that they were.

"Beats me," Daphne said airily. "Maybe the beaches are too dirty or everyone got bored. All I know is quite a few people are back already. Donny Montesquieu called me up just this morning looking for a few clever pieces for his new apartment and Ree-ree Klerck was getting her hair done the same time I was. She said Nepal was awful, by the way, nothing decent to buy and everyone so dirty."

"It's a very poor and oppressed country," Petra muttered, remembering her own visit there. She'd taken some of the best photos of her career. Ree-ree Klerck was an idiot.

"Giles mentioned something about getting out tonight," she said reluctantly. "Maybe a party." Hastily she added, "I told him there wouldn't be anything interesting, but he wanted me to try anyway."

"You should check your mail, sweetie," Daphne said. She had a little snigger under her breath, almost a chuckle, as though the mere notion of Petra doing something because a man wanted her to was almost too much to stand.

"Darling Daryl is throwing a little bash, and I know for a fact that he invited you."

Petra's heart sank. "Why would he do that? We didn't exactly part on the best of terms."

To put it mildly. Daryl had plain and simply gotten tired of a platonic relationship. So had every other man she'd ever tried to date up until Giles. But then, of course, he had neatly done away with the problem.

"I gather Daryl is filled with remorse and desperate to see you again," Daphne chortled. "I would have mentioned it before, but when you came home with that gorgeous hunk, I decided it was superfluous. However, if you're looking for a little fun...."

"I'm not. Besides, it sounds awful."

"What does?" Giles inquired genially. He had come into the bedroom, blithely ignoring the glare she gave him, and plopped down on the bed. If so elegant and graceful a man could ever be said to plop anywhere.

"Going on a liquid diet for six months," Petra said. "It's a powder made out of ground seaweed. You dissolve it in purified water and ..."

"Hi, Daphne," Giles said. He smiled contritely but otherwise offered no apology for taking over the phone.

"Hi, gorgeous," Daphne said. "Don't tell me you're bored already. You can't possibly be."

"Far from it," he replied. "I'm just looking for a little information, a better feel for things. What's the best party in town tonight?"

"The Comtesse de Langford is giving a little soirée for eighty of her most intimate friends, but that one promises to be a bit trite. Angelique is terribly sweet but she hasn't had an original thought since poodle skirts were in vogue."

"What else?"

"Let's see...several of the consulates are having bashes, but that will just be the usual people saying the usual things, eating the usual caviar. If you're in the mood for show biz, there are a couple of 'angel parties' for well-heeled investors eager to help float next season's flops. Or you could go to the little get-together Daryl Ellis is throwing. He's rented out the Patrice Lumumba Museum for a sixties party."

"Refresh my memory, Daphne. Why would anyone want to give a party to relive the 1960s? They're right up there with the plague years of the Dark Ages."

"You're showing your age, dear, or your education. Don't you know that everything that happened longer ago than last Monday is pure nostalgia?"

"Pure baloney, if you ask me, but we'll go." Ignoring Petra's frantic hand signals of rejection, he added, "However, I am absolutely not wearing bell-bottoms."

"Pity, you'd look marvelous. If I were a teeny bit younger... Ah, well...what will be and all that. Have a good time but don't—repeat don't—get into any mischief. I would not appreciate my star client—and dear, dear friend—being any further discomfited than she already has been."

"You and me both," Giles said. He evaded Petra's efforts to grab the phone and hung up. Pure male anticipation danced in his eyes as he said, "So good old Daryl's giving a party. How could we miss it?"

"Go to hell," Petra muttered. She stomped out of the bedroom and went into the kitchen, where she began aimlessly tossing dishes together for the sole purpose of making cold and hostile noises.

"Cut it out," Giles said mildly as he came up behind her. "You don't have all that many plates to start with. If you smash them, we'll have to eat out all the time. Besides, you're not really mad about this. You just don't like the idea of my taking charge."

"You're damn right I don't," Petra said. "What makes you think you can come in here, take over and start deciding what I'm going to be doing? I've run my life just fine, thank you very much, and I'll go right on running it. Furthermore, if you think that . . ."

"Hush," Giles said gently. Ignoring her resistance—admittedly confused and uncertain—he drew her to him. Holding her with infinite tenderness, he said, "It's all right, Petra. I'm not going to dominate you, and I'm not going to abandon you. I'm looking for some middle ground here, but you've got to help me find it."

She looked up at him slowly, her heart beating very fast. Her eyes were dark pools of doubt lit by flickers of hope.

"Is that what you're trying to do?" she murmured.

He nodded solemnly. "That's it. I admit I haven't had much practice, but I really am determined. Now if you don't want to go to the party, I can understand that. I'll go alone. Just as long as you understand that I'm not walking away from this. We're going to get to the bottom of what's been happening.''

"I guess it would be rude to let you go by yourself.''

"Let's just say it wouldn't be nice.''

"There's that word again.''

His eyebrows rose. "What word?''

"Nice. It keeps cropping up somehow.'' Unwilling to pursue that particular avenue of thought, she went on briskly, "All right, I'll go, but only for a drop-in. No way am I going to stand around all night listening to a bunch of retread hippies reminisce about the good old days.''

"Deal,'' Giles said. He dropped a quick kiss on her upturned lips, and then, just when she was beginning to think that he was really being very respectful of her personhood, he added a quick pat to the fanny.

"Get dressed, sweetheart,'' he said with an unrepentant grin, "we don't want to keep darling Daryl in suspense.''

## Chapter 13

The Patrice Lumumba Museum was located in a turn-of-the-century townhouse on East Twenty-third Street off Fifth Avenue. Formerly the residence of a textile merchant, the house had been inherited by his great-great-grandson, a sixties radical.

That young man was killed in 1971 while involved in the processing of nitroglycerin. Under the terms of his hotly disputed will, the townhouse became the possession of the Patrice Lumumba foundation, named for the black African revolutionary.

Apart from its name, the foundation had no obvious relation to blacks, Africa, revolution or much of anything else. Its stated purpose was to "document the cosmic unifying of the human spirit with the eternal and universal generative force."

Officially it was a museum. Effectively it was a catering hall.

"I've been to a party here once before," Petra said as they entered. "It was a Young Republicans fund-raiser sometime last year."

Giles glanced around at the stark white walls crisscrossed by lacquered streaks of black and orange, which drew the eye upward three stories to an atrium roof festooned with what appeared to be a giant nursery mobile.

"All right," he said, "I'll bite. One, why were you at a Young Rebpulicans fund-raiser, and two, why did they have it here?"

"One," she said with a grin, "I was doing a piece on social climbing through politics. No offense to the Young Republicans, but it was an obvious place to start. Two, I understand this place is relatively cheap, has great space, and they do a thing with smoked salmon platters that everyone swears is fantastic. I can't personally vouch for that because I was too busy working the last time to get a taste, but maybe we'll find out tonight."

"I live in anticipation," Giles murmured. He sidestepped a couple dressed in what looked like the plumage of exotic—and probably extinct—birds, and guided Petra toward what appeared to be the main room. This single space ran the entire length of the house from front to back. Originally it would have comprised the parlor, dining room and family sitting room, but no trace of its former existence remained other than the high ceiling.

Giles grimaced as he glanced around. "This place has been gutted. There was no attempt at preservation. All the moldings are gone, along with the fireplace mantels, the window sashes, even the flooring. It's really a shame."

"Until recently, people just didn't value those things," Petra reminded him gently. "They were more interested in tearing down and starting over than they were in restoring."

The look he shot her made it clear what he thought of that. They accepted fluted glasses of champagne from a passing waiter. When the man had gone on with his carefully balanced silver tray, Giles laughed.

"All these people trying to prove how with-it they are, but they still want waiters dressed up in tuxedos passing out champagne, just as they would have been doing a hundred years ago."

"You're saying we're all rooted in the past whether we want to admit it or not?" Petra asked. She didn't much like the idea of that, given her own experience, but she was more willing to consider it than she ever had been before.

"Exactly." Bluntly he added, "It's the people who try to deny it who end up in trouble."

She looked around her at the glittering array of stylish, with-it men and women absorbed in themselves and in the moment. All of them were striving to be different, memorable, to stand out in some way and to attract attention. And yet they were amazingly alike—slender, perfectly groomed and young. She caught snatches of conversations she had heard a hundred times before—the latest hot artist, stock, real estate, vacation spot, food, drink, designer, whatever. The names changed, everything else stayed the same.

The noise level was high, everyone trying to be heard above everyone else. Raucous laughter broke out frequently, the goal being to project the notion that everyone was having a fabulous time because, after all, how could they not, what with being so young, attractive and with-it.

Petra's hand inched up automatically toward the camera that for once was not hanging around her neck. She had deliberately left it at home. Without the protection it offered, she felt disconcertingly vulnerable. Hardly realizing that she did so, she slipped her hand through Giles's arm.

"There's Daryl," she said.

He raised his eyebrows at her obvious relief. "That's a thrill."

"Oh, stop," she admonished. "I just meant that we can say 'hi,' stay a few minutes and leave."

"We'll see," he said noncommittally as he began cutting their way through the crowd to reach their host.

Daryl saw them coming. He flashed a quick, dismissive smile at the redhead he'd been talking to and headed in their direction.

Petra stifled a sigh. There had been a time not too long ago when she'd believed that Daryl would be the man to release her from the sterility of her own emotions and enable her to experience life more fully. Even now, with the benefit of hindsight, she could well understand why she felt that way.

He was classically handsome with thick blond hair, aquiline features and a slender but muscular body. As tall as Giles but less powerfully built, he projected a far lighter and less physical aura. Where Giles was a man she could easily imagine tackling the toughest and most dangerous jobs, Daryl had "boardroom" practically stamped on his forehead. Also "private club," "yacht" and "East Side duplex."

A child of old money, he had made a name for himself on Wall Street in the rah-rah eighties. More recently he'd gone out on his own, forming a consortium to advise on mergers and acquisitions. Petra had no idea how well the business was going, but Daryl showed every evidence of continued prosperity.

His energy had always astounded her. Whereas she could work for long periods when she was in the throes of a special project, Daryl did it routinely. He customarily rose in the wee hours of the morning to catch the London opening and then stayed with it as the day aged and the flow of commerce spread across the globe, ending up finally across the international dateline in Tokyo. He talked enthusiastically of the day when there would truly be a world market, operating twenty-four hours a day, seven days a week, girding the globe in a single, vast, ultimate *deal*.

"Petra," he said, holding out both hands to her. He dropped a quick kiss on her cheek and gazed at her in gentle reprimand. "I've been going crazy trying to reach you, babe. Where have you been?"

She took a quick step back, disentangling herself. His show of affection embarrassed her. She didn't want Giles to get the wrong impression.

"Out of town," she said quickly. "Daryl, I'd like you to meet a friend of mine, Professor Giles Chastain. Giles, this is Daryl Ellis."

The two men eyed each other cautiously. Daryl flashed an easy smile. "Nice to meet you, Professor. I'm glad you could come along tonight. There are some people here I think you'd like to meet."

Chatting lightly, he led them in the direction of a statuesque brunette who was holding court in one corner.

"Melinda, darling, this is Giles Chastain, *Professor* Chastain, that is. Of course, you know Petra."

Melinda darling smiled coolly at Petra and turned her considerable charms on Giles. "Such a surprise," she purred, "to meet a man here with any claim to intellectual achievement. Daryl and his ilk are amazingly lightweight and proud of it."

"Melinda's a terrible snob," Daryl said pleasantly. "She can't get over the fact that she speaks seven languages and has four master's degrees. Or is it four languages and seven..."

"Scat, sweetie. The Professor and I have things to talk about." She laid a proprietorial hand on Giles's arm and smiled incandescently.

Petra was about to say something both crude and rude when Giles shot her a warning glance. He returned Melinda's smile with full force and suggested they get a drink.

"That's taken care of," Daryl said as he led Petra off in the opposite direction. Blissfully ignoring the fire spitting from her eyes, he murmured, "Really,

darling, what were you thinking of bringing somebody like that along? He's not our sort at all.''

"I thought he wasn't," Petra agreed tightly. "Now
I'm wondering." What on earth could have inspired
Giles to go off with the insipid Melinda? Worse yet,
why had he so readily stepped aside and left her with
Daryl?

"I've missed you, darling," Daryl was saying. He
gazed down at her fondly. "You can't know how
much. It was such a bummer, not being able to see
you."

"I thought we'd agreed that was best," Petra said.
"It was obvious that we weren't headed anywhere together, and then you took up with Babushka."

"Birishka," he corrected. "She was a terrible mistake, a total air-head, if you know what I mean. I
swear, that woman never had a thought in her head
beyond what she was going to wear and how great she
looked."

Since Daryl had never evinced any more than the
most superficial interest in anybody's thoughts, Petra
was hard-pressed to see how their lack would have
been a deterrent.

Pointedly she said, "She seemed perfect for you."

"Only on the surface, darling. It was because we
looked so good together, everyone was fooled. But
you and I..." His voice dropped, becoming low and
seductive. "Oh, I know we've never been as close as
I'd like but that's just because you're old-fashioned.
I under—"

"I'm what?" Petra broke in. Of all the terms she
might have accepted to describe herself, old-fashioned

was definitely not one of them. Repressed, maybe. Screwed-up, possibly, although not on a good day. And besides, that was all in the past, thanks to Giles. But old-fashioned most certainly did not describe her. It never had.

Had it?

"Old-fashioned," Daryl repeated, blissfully unaware of her reaction. "That's fine, really. I respect it. It's very refreshing after all this poor society of ours has been through. You and I just need more time together, we have to work at getting to know each other better."

He spoke with the deathless conviction of a man who has just discovered an ultimate truth, one he presumes everyone else has missed.

Petra shook her head as another glass of champagne was proffered her way and stared at him skeptically. "This is quite a change for you, Daryl. If you don't mind my saying so, I had the impression that you simply weren't willing to give so much time or effort to a relationship."

"That was a failing on my part," he agreed hastily. "But it's all in the past. We'll start fresh, and you'll see how much better it will be." As though suddenly struck by the happy thought, he added, "Let's begin this evening. We can have dinner together at that new place, Eats, then we can go on to the cabaret show at Villiers. We'll have a great time, you'll see."

Petra swallowed hard. She hated hurting anyone's feelings, but Daryl made it particularly hard. His eyes were wide and ingenuous. A lock of golden hair fell across his high brow. He looked like an especially handsome little boy pleading for an extra cookie. Or like a nice purebred whippet wanting a cuddle.

"I'm sorry," she said softly. "Giles and I have plans."

Daryl looked at her dumbly for a moment, as though what she had said simply didn't compute. When the words finally sank in, he smiled.

"Darling, I'm sorry to disappoint you, but Melinda the Marvelous has your Professor well in tow. They disappeared not two minutes after I introduced them."

Petra whirled around. The spot where Giles had been standing with Melinda was indeed empty; neither of them was anywhere to be seen.

"There must be some mistake," Petra murmured.

"You can never trust those academic types," Daryl said as he took her arm again. "Now, I have to touch base with a few people. Why don't you help yourself to the salmon, it really is marvelous. But don't spoil your appetite. You want to be hungry when we get to Eats."

What she wanted, Petra thought dourly, was to punch out a certain professor of British history who was definitely getting too big for his britches. How dare he do such a thing to her? Of all the insensitive, unfeeling, thoughtless...

Daryl was right, the salmon was good. She stood there, beside the buffet table, defiantly eating a good deal more of it than she should have while she shot glares at the four corners of the room. So Giles was gone, good. She could get over this stupid illusion she'd been having about true love and happily-ever-after. She'd dump his stuff on the sidewalk for him to find and get back to real life. She'd—

Giles was back, striding easily through the crowd straight toward her. She turned away hastily, determined not to let him see the anguished look in her eyes. She stiffened as his hand reached past her to claim a small slice of Brie.

"Sorry that took so long," he said. "Everything all right?"

"Sorry... what are you talking about?"

"I didn't mean to stick you with Daryl, but it was just too good an opportunity to pass up."

"An opportunity for what?" Petra demanded. "Or shouldn't I ask?"

Giles stared at her for a long moment, taking in her fiery sapphire eyes and the high color of her cheeks. Slowly he smiled. "You're jealous."

"Jealous?" she repeated, her voice rising an octave. "I've never been jealous in my life, you insufferable boor. How dare you think that I'd care anything about what you do?"

His smile deepening, he bent his tall head and dropped a light kiss on her outraged lips. "That's sweet," he said. "I like your being jealous, but don't let it get out of hand. It's totally unjustified."

Petra looked up at him through the thick screen of her lashes. Her entire body was tingling from his touch, but she would have been drawn and quartered before letting him know that. "It is?"

"I wanted to know something about good ol' Daryl and his crowd, and Melinda offered a quick way to find it out. She couldn't have been more obliging."

"I'll bet," Petra muttered.

"I hadn't been talking with her more than a few minutes when she very generously suggested that we do a few lines."

Petra's eyes widened. She had the sudden sense of stepping outside of herself into a terrifyingly unknown realm. "L-lines?"

Giles looked at her chidingly. "I thought you were with-it, modern, in the swim. The chronicler of our society, isn't that what the *Times* called you?"

"*Chronicler*," she said hoarsely. "Not necessarily a participant. As you may have noticed, I've never been too good at that part."

"Oh, I don't know, you seem to do fine, at least so far as I'm concerned." His smile softened as he saw her continued distress.

"I don't understand," Petra said. "I thought I knew these people. Sure drug use is widespread, but to be that blatant about it is just plain stupid. I thought Melinda was supposed to be pretty smart."

"I think all that business about languages and degrees may be just one more drug-induced fantasy," Giles said gently. "But smart or not, she's definitely a user."

"I wonder if Daryl knows," Petra mused softly. "He's known Melinda a long time, maybe he could help her."

"Hmmm," Giles said. "Let's get going."

"We should find Daryl again to say goodbye."

"It won't break his heart if we don't."

"I don't want to be like that," Petra demurred. "He...was very nice about everything."

Giles shot her a hard, penetrating look. "I'll just bet he was. Let's go."

"You're very arbitrary," she said when they were standing outside the front door. "Did anyone ever mention that to you?"

The wind lifted his hair, softening the hard contours of his face. "Never. Everybody says I'm a real pussycat."

He lifted his hand, signaling for a cab. Petra bit back a smile. It was the late evening rush hour when everyone was hurrying to and from parties. In addition, it was starting to rain. By an absolutely inviolate New York law it was impossible to get a cab.

One screeched to a halt directly in front of them. "Where to, sir?" the cabbie inquired.

Sir? Petra had never heard a cab driver say anything remotely like that. They were given to far more informal and earthy forms of address.

"How did you do that?" she muttered as they settled into the back of the cab.

Giles gave the driver her address. He put an arm around her. Instinctively she snuggled closer.

"Magic," he said.

# Chapter 14

It was not magic but a miracle of modern technology that awaited them back at the loft. Petra's fax machine had spewed out an answer to the inquiry Giles had sent to Washington.

He studied it as she fixed coffee. She brought the tray into the living room, where they sat together. Silently he handed her the sheet of paper.

She saw a grainy photograph of a man who looked very much like the hard-faced man she had caught at the party. But this man was obviously younger and more casually dressed, in an open-necked white shirt and trousers. He stood in front of what looked like a tropical background.

"Does the name Pacorro Grillas mean anything to you?" Giles asked.

Petra shook her head. "Nothing. Is that his name?"

"So it seems. It looks as though Paul really came through. Incidentally there are some people on their way here to talk with you."

"What people?"

"Agents from the Drug Enforcement Administration. It seems that Pacorro Grillas is one of the world's largest drug dealers. He escaped the Colombian crackdown in '89 and was believed to be hiding in Panama. But he moves around a lot, and no one is ever sure where he is. There are no fewer than forty outstanding warrants for his arrest in this country alone. If he ever sets foot in the U.S., he's dog meat."

"Then this can't be him," Petra insisted. "I photographed this man right here in New York less than a month ago."

"Which is exactly why the DEA men want to talk to you."

Petra was still insisting that something had to be wrong when the men arrived. Both were young, somber and scrupulously polite. They were also determined.

"We understand what you're saying, Ms. O'Toole," the one who identified himself as Bert said. "It is highly unlikely that Pacorro Grillas would enter this country. However, he is known to be very stubborn and flamboyant. He might do it simply to flaunt his ability to evade arrest."

"Which he seems to have accomplished," Giles cut in. "You had no other indication that he could be here?"

The men glanced at each other. Bert remained silent as the other, called Dave, said, "There have been rumors, Professor Chastain, but nothing hard enough to go on. Even now, all we know is that Grillas was here a few weeks ago. The odds are that he's long gone."

"Then why are you here," Petra asked, "talking to me?"

"Because we understand you've had some trouble. We think there's a good possibility that Grillas has been trying to get hold of this photograph and its negative. He's flamboyant all right, but he isn't stupid. If he realized his visit here was being documented, he'd move heaven and earth to get hold of that evidence."

"Which means," Giles said curtly, "that since he hasn't succeeded in doing that, Petra is still in danger."

The drug agents hesitated. Finally Bert said, "That's about the size of it, Ms. O'Toole. We're fully prepared to get word to Grillas that the photograph is now in our possession. At the very least, that should cause him to back off. But in the meantime, it would be a good idea if you could make yourself scarce."

Petra looked at them both. She was fighting a growing sense of unreality. This couldn't be happening to her. It was like something out of a TV melodrama—photographer hunted by drug dealer. Only it was horribly, vividly real.

"I see," she said slowly. "Where do you suggest I go?"

"We have safe houses," Bert began.

"She's coming with me," Giles said. He raised a hand before anyone could object. "The tourist season is almost over on Block Island. In a few more days, any stranger there will stick out like a sore thumb. And my house is situated off by itself; no one can reach it without being seen."

"All the same, Professor," Dave said, "we think Ms. O'Toole would be safer with us. After all, we're the professionals at this sort of thing." His smile was just a shade patronizing.

"How many drug informers do you have in protective custody right now?" Giles demanded. "A dozen... two dozen? However many it is, I'm willing to bet that your resources are strained to the limit. As well-intentioned as you are, you can't offer any guarantees that your way will work."

"That's true," Bert murmured, "but all the same—"

"If you don't mind," Petra interjected. "This is my well-being we're talking about. I think I should have some say in it." She looked at each of the men. The drug agents looked worried but confident. Giles looked angry and ready to fight.

Quietly she said, "I'll go with Professor Chastain."

"Really, sweetheart," he said a few hours later, "there's no need to be so formal. You can call me Giles."

"You didn't look like a Giles just then," Petra shot back. "You looked every inch the outraged professor confronted with not-very-bright students. I wouldn't have dared cross you."

"Smart attitude," he said. "Those guys mean well; they're just being pulled in too many directions at the same time. I trust them to get the word to Grillas, but that's about all."

"Do you really think that will do it?" Petra asked. She couldn't help but be worried. The idea of being the target of a drug kingpin's attentions was terrifying.

"I talked with Paul Delacroix while you were packing," Giles said. "The word on Grillas is that he considers himself a businessman. He doesn't believe in a lot of wasted effort. Besides, if Bert and Ernie—sorry, Bert and Dave—are right and he wanted to make a point, he'll be satisfied that he's gotten it across."

Petra frowned; there was something wrong with the logic of that. "If he really wanted government authorities to know he was here, why did he try to steal the photograph?"

"I don't know," Giles admitted. He cursed himself silently for having brought up the point. Petra was too smart to fall for a line of reasoning like that. She suspected the whole thing smelled and she was right.

"Anyway," he went on quickly, "we'll be home soon."

Home. Petra tried the word out in her own mind. Oddly enough, it seemed to fit.

She was tired by the time Giles maneuvered the Land Rover off the ferry. The quiet of the island after the noise of New York was almost stunning. Although it was still more crowded than it would be shortly, the island seemed like an oasis of sanity and serenity.

She breathed in deeply, savoring the cool salt air, and smiled. "It's good to be back."

They stopped at the store to pick up supplies for dinner. Once at the house, they opened all the windows to let out the musty smell, then unpacked quickly. Giles gave his mail a cursory glance before adjourning to the kitchen.

Several hours later, sated by linguine, salad and scampi, Petra was hard-pressed to keep her eyes open. She was only vaguely aware when Giles slid her between the cool, smooth sheets.

"Nice," she murmured drowsily.

He dropped a light kiss on her forehead. "Very. Go to sleep now."

She needed no further encouragement to fall away into blissful forgetfulness.

Sometime toward dawn she woke from a dream of men chasing her while somewhere nearby another laughed derisively. She was lying in Giles's arms, close enough to feel the steadiness of his heartbeat beneath her cheek. For a moment, the terror of the dream clung to her like a cloying cloud. Then the warmth and security of the bed—and the man—dispelled it.

Giles was deeply asleep. He lay on his back, his arms around her, his legs akimbo. The hard lines of his face were relaxed. His lips were slightly parted.

Petra smiled softly. She was discovering on a personal level what she had heard about but never before experienced—there was something about a sleeping man that brought out a confusion of feelings in a woman, part sexy, part maternal, all tender.

Awake, he was indomitably assured and capable. Asleep, he was far more vulnerable and approachable.

She hesitated a moment before making up her mind. Perhaps she'd change it and not wake him after all, but it wouldn't hurt to make a quick trip to the bathroom just to brush her teeth and add a splash of perfume.

Slowly, careful not to disturb him prematurely, she slipped from his arms. The floor was cool beneath her feet. She moved around it and was headed for the bathroom when Giles came suddenly, shockingly awake.

One moment she was standing upright under her own power, the next she was flat on her back on the floor, a steel-hard forearm pressed against her throat and her breath cut off.

"Oh, God," Giles said. Just as quickly, she was released. Still stunned by what had happened, reeling from the impact of it, she was hardly aware of being dragged upright and examined from head to toe.

"Petra," he entreated urgently, "speak to me. Did I hurt you? Are you all right?"

She stared at him mutely, her eyes huge and filled with bewilderment. He cursed under his breath and lifted her quickly, laying her on the bed. A moment later, he was kneeling beside her gently soothing her face with a damp cloth.

"Petra...I'm sorry...I had no idea what I was doing..."

"W-what—" She sounded like a flu-ridden frog. Having cleared her throat, she said, "I'm fine, it's okay. I was just a little...surprised." Gathering steam, she added, "What happened to you? One minute you were peacefully asleep and the next you were acting like some combination of Rambo and Ninja warrior. It was just me going to the bathroom."

"I know, I'm sorry...that is, I didn't know. I just heard footsteps and I woke up. I wasn't thinking...." He looked at her abashedly. "I guess I'm a little tense about this business with Grillas."

"I'd hate to see you really stressed-out," Petra muttered. She regretted the words almost immediately. Giles looked so truly regretful and embarrassed that her heart turned over.

"Hey," she said softly, ruffling his hair, "it's not a big thing. Actually it's kind of interesting. I had no idea you had such great reflexes."

Giles grimaced, tried to turn it into a smile, and half succeeded. He wouldn't—couldn't—tell her that the reflexes were another legacy of China, where he'd learned to sleep constantly attuned to danger. But he could—and did—appreciate her efforts to smooth over what had happened.

"Not so great," he said thickly, vividly aware of her slender body so close to his own. "I'm afraid I hurt you." In fact, he was afraid he was about to. His desire for her was suddenly so rampant that he doubted his ability to control it. Something about the shock of danger had triggered a need to possess her that went beyond anything he had yet experienced.

Petra seemed unaware of the effect she was having. She lay before him, shielded only by the thin ivory silk of her nightgown, and smiled gently.

"I'm fine," she murmured as her arm rose in a graceful arc, her fingers gently smoothing the hair she had ruffled. "There's no harm done."

"That's good." He lifted himself above her, sitting on the edge of the bed, and fought the temptation to touch her. "You should go back to sleep."

"Why?"

"You just should."

She laughed softly. "You'll have to do better than that. I'm feeling wide awake."

Also suddenly warm and acutely conscious of the feel of silk brushing her skin. It should have been pleasant, but instead the touch of fabric was almost unbearable. So was the distance between her and Giles. She desperately needed to be as close to him as she possibly could be.

"Giles . . . ?"

"What is it, Petra?"

"Don't you think you ought to get back into bed?"

"Ah...no...I'm not really sleepy right now. I'll just go downstairs and get some work done. You go to sleep."

He started to rise, only to be stopped by her hand on his arm. Her touch burned him to the core of his being. He could feel the heavy thud of his heart and the sudden heated pooling of desire in his loins.

"Actually, I'm not sleepy, either."

"You're not?"

"No," she said solemnly.

"I'll fix you some warm milk. That will help relax you."

She could think of something a whole lot better that would relax her a whole lot faster. Further, she was willing to bet her best Nikon that Giles felt the same way. Too bad he was set on being so damned Victorian.

Or maybe it wasn't. It might be fun to shake him out of it.

She put a hand to her forehead, closed her eyes, and emoted. "Ohhh..."

He leaned forward at once. She felt the tiniest twinge of guilt that was promptly washed away by the thought that this was really for his own good.

"I don't think warm milk will really help, Giles, though it's so sweet of you to offer. I'm just feeling all... I don't know exactly... tingly..."

"It must be shock," he said. "You're breaking out in goose bumps."

That was because he was running his hands down her bare arms, sending up delicious little pathways of erotic excitement. But if he wanted to think it was shock, fine.

"That must be it. I just can't stand the idea of being alone. Could you please hold me?"

Where was the man who could resist such an entreaty? Not in Giles Chastain's bedroom, that was for sure. He wasted no time rejoining her in the bed, drawing her close against his hard, bare chest and murmuring to her soothingly.

Under other circumstances—say, for instance, if she'd been five years old—Petra could have gone blissfully to sleep. In fact, she felt a momentary twinge of regret that Giles hadn't been around when she was a child in sore need of such comfort.

Of course, being a fully grown woman had its compensations.

As she was being reminded when Giles's hand moved slowly down her back to the curve of her hip. He turned on his side, then hesitated before bringing her fully under him.

He said nothing, nor did she expect him to. The feeling was too powerful, the need too immediate. It went beyond all reason and sense into a realm where neither of those faculties could function.

Where there was only the fierce strength and proud passion of their intertwining bodies; the slither of silk as it moved away from skin; the deep, almost reverent murmur of a male voice; the scent of night air rising on the heat of desire; and the soft cries of a woman catapulted into fulfillment.

Afterward, there was the perfumed benediction of wild grasses casting their seeds on the warm breezes that fluttered the old lace curtains and set them to dancing like unabashed phantasms of ancient memory celebrating the sheer, unbridled, foot-stomping, voice-raising triumph of man and woman coming, against all odds, to love each other.

In the morning, there was nothing so pretty.

Petra woke to hammering. Brash, merciless sunlight flooded the room. Far from dancing, the curtains hung uselessly at either side of the open windows.

She groaned, turned over, jerked a pillow over her head and tried to sink back down into marshmallowy unconsciousness. Only to encounter the rock-hard resistance of her own senses.

*Bang-bang . . . bam-bam . . . bang-bang . . .*

It went on that way for several minutes until Petra jerked her head up, flung the pillow onto the floor and glowered darkly toward the windows.

That had no effect whatsoever on the hammering, which continued unabated, but it made her feel better to get angry.

A glance at the clock confirmed that it was barely 8:00 *a.m.* Heaven knew, Giles had many oustanding virtues—more than a few of which he had demonstrated yet again the night before. But the man had to be suicidal to wake her up this way at such an ungodly hour.

Except that it wasn't Giles who was responsible for the cacophony. As Petra discovered when she emerged, wrapped in a silk kimono emblazoned with a full-figured dragon that she had stuffed into her bag back in New York.

Two young men were straddling ladders up toward the roof of the house. Two more were on the roof itself. All four wore jeans, grins and nothing else. As soon as they caught sight of the bare-footed dragon with the tidal wave of unruly red hair, they whistled appreciatively.

Petra sighed, turned on her heel and went back inside. She found Giles downstairs. He was talking with an older man who nodded to Petra and quickly made himself scarce.

"What's going on?" she asked.

Giles hesitated a split second. He was dressed in his usual khaki pants and old cotton shirt left open at the neck. His hair still glistened from a recent shower. Memories of the night flowed through her, heightening the color bathing her cheeks.

"I'm having a little work done on the house," Giles said finally. His eyes swept over her tenderly, but he sounded unrepentant when he added, "Sorry if the noise woke you."

Petra shot him a skeptical look before helping herself to a cup of coffee from the pot he'd fixed. She took a sip before she asked, "What kind of work?"

"Some renovation up along the roof, a few other things, nothing big. What do you say we get out of here while this is going on? We could take a picnic out to the bluffs. It looks like a great day."

The sky was crystal clear, the breeze balmy, the air pure. He was absolutely right; any person in her right mind would want to be outside.

Petra needed three full sips of coffee to convince herself that it was even an option. And then she waffled.

"I'll make you a deal," she said grudgingly. "You tell me what those men are really doing up on the roof and I'll seriously consider picnicking."

Giles looked at her chidingly. "I'm not sure that's an even swap. What's so tough about a picnic?"

"I've had a New York-fix. I'm back in the mode where going outside is never an absolutely great idea, much less sitting on the dirt to eat food."

"Uh-oh, back to nature-phobia. I thought we'd gotten you past that, but okay, I'll bite. The men on the roof are putting in floodlights."

"Authentic turn-of-the-century Victorian floodlights, I hope?" she demanded sarcastically.

"State of the art photovoltaic phosphorescent floodlights."

"How are we going to sleep with them on?"

Giles looked at her bemusedly. "Is that all you think of, sleeping?"

"No, sometimes I think of how incredibly dumb a certain man can be." Hands on her hips, chin up, eyes flaming, Petra said, "This is going entirely too far. I should never have let you convince me to come back here. You're taking on way too much responsibility for my safety. If you really believe the situation is so bad that you need floodlights strung up around your house, then I have no business being here."

Her voice broke. She looked away hastily, consumed with the sudden stark fear that she had spent the last several days doing her best to avoid. Now it crashed down on her relentlessly. Fear not only for herself—she could have coped with that—but fear for Giles. The pulse-pounding, stomach-churning fear for another that laid bare the true extent of her vulnerability and made a mockery of all her vaunted claims of independence.

His hand on her shoulder steadied her. Gently, not saying anything, he drew her against him. His breath was warm on her skin as he murmured, "Stop trying to run, Petra. You're right where you belong."

# Chapter 15

"Tell me about Daryl."

Petra opened her eyes slowly. She was lying on the blanket stretched out on an open patch of ground above the bluffs. Beneath lay the magnificently eroded cliffs, the rock-strewn beach and the white-flecked sea. Above, the sky continued blatantly cloudless, dazzling in its perfection.

None of which had anything whatsoever to do with Daryl Ellis. So why had Giles suddenly mentioned him?

"Daryl who?" she murmured, hoping he'd get the hint and drop the subject.

He did and he didn't. Stretching out beside her, his head propped in the palm of his hand, he smiled gently. "*Daryl* Daryl. How did you meet him?"

"We were actually found together as infants on a stretch of interstate highway near Giants Stadium. We were raised by wolves indigenous to the New Jersey meadowlands. Later we separated when I joined a traveling group of Amway salesmen and Daryl entered politics. Years passed before we encountered each other again at a pickle shop on Broome Street and discovered that we had both spent the intervening time learning Wagnerian arias at a small music school off Eighth Avenue. Enough said?"

He laughed, although not for very long. "Cute. Now for real, how did you meet him?"

"At some gallery opening—I don't remember the details. We knew each other for a while before we tried dating."

"Did you date for long?"

She shook her head. The sun was pleasantly warm on her closed eyelids. It seemed easier to go along with him.

"A few weeks. I was trying to... make a change in myself. I was tired of being..."

"A virgin?"

She heard the smile in his voice but refused to acknowledge it. "I just thought it was time I tried breaking out of the cocoon I seemed to have woven for myself."

"And you thought Daryl was the man to do it with?" The smile was gone. It was clear what he thought of that notion.

"He's very attractive," she pointed out defensively. "Well educated, well off, well positioned. What more could a girl ask for?"

"So what went wrong?"

"I don't know," she admitted. "He was fun to go around with, but every place we went, I seemed to end up working. We never stayed by ourselves, getting to know each other. Daryl didn't seem to feel any need for that, and I had no idea how to initiate it."

"It's called intimacy," Giles said, "and it's true, it is tough."

"Oh, Daryl wasn't averse to being intimate," Petra said wryly. "He just seemed to think that we could come back from some big bash where we'd spent the evening surrounded by a hundred other people and jump straight into bed. I couldn't do it, it was that simple. I needed to get to know him first, and I never got the chance."

Even as she said the words she realized how true they were. If anyone had asked her if she "knew" Daryl Ellis, she would have automatically said yes. But in fact, all she knew was his name, a few details about his background, his obsession with his work, and so on. The man himself—that complex and contradictory bundle of wants, needs, fears and hopes that makes everyone unique—was completely closed off from her.

"So after a few weeks you went your separate ways?" Giles asked.

Petra nodded. "He took up with Babushka—sorry, Birishka—and I just kept on working."

Giles fell silent. He stretched out on his back beside her. Their bodies touched closely enough so that she could feel his continued alertness. Silent he might be, but she knew his mind was whirling away.

"Why are you so interested in Daryl?" she asked.

Instead of answering her directly, Giles said, "Did he invite you to that party in the hopes of getting back together?"

"Uh, well . . . actually—"

"He did."

"It's not a big deal," she added hastily. "Besides, he was very sweet about it. I still feel badly about leaving the party without saying goodbye to him."

Giles grunted noncommittally. He fell silent again, leaving Petra to her own thoughts. His interest in Daryl surprised her, but she chalked it up to typical male competitiveness. She even felt a tiny twinge of female satisfaction, which she tried virtuously to ignore.

By the time they'd returned to the house in the early afternoon, the men had finished their work and gone. Petra stood on the front lawn by the ancient oak tree and looked up at the roof. She couldn't restrain a grimace.

"They look fine," Giles said.

"They stick out like Dumbo's ears."

He put an arm around her shoulders and hugged her gently. "You're exaggerating. Besides, I've been meaning to have this done for a while."

Petra looked at him skeptically. "Why?"

"So I can find this place in the fog. You must have noticed, there are no other houses right around here. We get real pea-soupers that can last a couple of days. The last time it happened, I went out to the store and was hardly able to find my way back. With these lights, I won't have that problem."

Petra remained skeptical, but she was grateful to him for claiming that the lights had some purpose beyond the present situation.

The remainder of that day and all of the following passed quietly. They stayed largely at home, working in companionable silence, cooking together and making love in the immense sleigh bed. When they did go out, it was as a couple—to shop at the BIG, grab a hamburger at the Harborside Inn or stop by the library.

They might have been honeymooners or even old married people who had retained a gratifying measure of affection for each other. Remembering her earlier feeling of isolation, Petra couldn't help but prefer the change. Nature and society both seemed to decree that humans come in twos. She had spent her life bucking that. Now that she had finally caved in, the rewards were proving even greater than she could have imagined.

But so were the drawbacks. By the third day, she was overdosing on togetherness. When Giles blithely suggested that they take *Feng-p'o-p'o* out, she demurred.

"I need to work."

"You worked most of yesterday," he pointed out reasonably. "It won't hurt you to take a break."

Petra hesitated. He was being so damn kind and considerate, so pleasant and easygoing, so "nice." By contrast, she felt shrewish and thoroughly unpleasant, but she couldn't seem to help it.

"I don't take breaks when my work is going well," she said. "I need to stay with it."

"All right," he said. "I've got things I can do myself."

He went off, seemingly unperturbed, to organize his papers and get down to work. Petra breathed a sigh of relief. Maybe this wasn't so bad after all. She started in again on the seemingly endless task of selecting pictures and was making some headway when, fifteen minutes later, Giles came back into the living room.

"You've got to see this," he said.

She glanced at the copy of *The New Yorker* he held out to her. The magazine was noted for its witty, startling and sometimes just plain bizarre cartoons. Petra usually enjoyed them, and she liked the one Giles showed her. But she wanted to get back to work.

"That's good," she said, handing him the magazine.

He left, she got back in the groove, and once again, everything seemed to go well. At least for half an hour or so.

"What do you want for lunch?" Giles asked, popping his head in again.

"Lunch? It's not even 10:00 a.m."

"I know," he said, "but I thought I'd defrost some cold soup. Is that all right with you?"

"Sure, sure, whatever you want."

After that, no matter how hard she tried, she couldn't blot out her awareness of him. First, she heard him moving around in the kitchen, then in his own study. He used an old electric typewriter that had a particularly high-pitched drone. The sound had never really bothered her before, but now it seemed to go straight through her skull.

Toward noon, just about when she was seriously considering gathering up all the photos and retreating to the attic, the phone rang. She heard Giles speaking quietly, listening at considerable length, asking questions. Finally he hung up.

This time when he came into the living room, it was without any hint of apology.

"That was Paul Delacroix in Washington," he said.

Petra sat cross-legged on the floor in front of a low inlaid table. Her eyes widened as she looked up at him. Apprehension darted through her.

"What did he say?"

"Nothing bad," Giles assured her quickly. "His people have been able to confirm that Grillas knows that the DEA has the photo." He hesitated a moment before he went on. "It seems he's pretty philosophical about it. The contact claimed he was actually amused."

"That's great," Petra exclaimed. "Then we can stop worrying about him."

A shadow flicked across Giles's hard face. "Yeah, maybe."

She jumped up, crossed the room and hugged him. "What a relief. We should celebrate."

Giles didn't have any problem with that. Especially not when the woman in his arms looked so heart-stoppingly carefree and beautiful. The strain he had felt growing in her over the past few days was gone. Not for the world would he do anything to restore it.

"All right," he said. They went out for lunch to a restaurant on Water Street specializing in fresh seafood with a southwestern touch that worked unexpectedly well. The food was superb, the service excellent and the wine tempting.

If Giles seemed subdued throughout the meal, Petra feigned not to notice. Liberated of her fears about Grillas, she presumed the problem of too much togetherness had also been solved. It was safe once again to fully enjoy Giles.

She was still in a pleasantly rosy frame of mind when they returned to the house. Laughing at something Giles had said, she stumbled over the doorstep but was saved from falling by the iron strength of his arm.

The breath rushed from her. She raised her head, finding his lips very close. It seemed the most natural thing in the world to touch her mouth to his.

Giles stood perfectly still. He neither moved further toward her nor away, but left matters entirely in her hands. Petra was momentarily taken aback but recovered quickly. A heady sense of freedom emboldened her.

His mouth was firm, warm and tasted slightly of the crisp chardonnay they had shared. Her fingers brushed over his lean jaw, tracing the beginning roughness that by the next morning would be enough to scratch her skin. Now it was only pleasantly arousing.

She raised herself on her toes and kissed him once, twice, lightly and teasingly, until that was not enough. Tentatively her tongue played along the ridge of his teeth. For a moment, she feared he would deny her, but then his lips parted slightly and a groan broke from him.

Their tongues thrust and parried in powerful evocation of the greater intimacy to come. Petra's hands trembled as she undid the buttons of his shirt. When she had spread it apart she tore her mouth from his and trailed hot, thirsting kisses along his broad chest. The flat male nipples hardened beneath her touch. His breath was ragged as he grasped her hips and held her to him.

"Much more of this," he said huskily, "and we will put Great-aunt Emmeline's entry hall to a use she never had in mind."

"How do you know?" Petra replied, fumbling with the buckle of his belt. "She sounds like she was quite a gal." Beneath the fabric of his slacks, she could feel his urgency and was excited by it. Her power to arouse him delighted her. She felt freer and more daring than ever before.

He made a sound deep in his throat that might have been agreement. Abruptly he lifted her, carrying her a few short paces to the heavy mahogany table against the wall.

"I hope you really want this, sweetheart," he said hotly, "because it's too damn late to stop."

Her gasp of pleasure when his big hands pulled up her skirt was all the assent he needed. Hastily, driven by need that allowed nothing for the niceties, they clung to each other. Giles stripped away her panties as her fingers tremblingly undid his fly. He lifted her quickly, positioning her, before bringing them together with shattering completeness.

His deep, powerful thrusts drove her quickly to incandescent pleasure. Her head fell back, the fiery hair pouring over his arms, as her throat tightened. Though she struggled to suppress it, in the final moment a scream of ecstasy broke from her, echoed by Giles's own husky shout.

For long moments, neither of them moved. Only slowly did they disentangle themselves and straighten their clothing. Petra was stunned by her own abandon. Their previous lovemaking had been exactly that—an exquisite, languorous drawing out of passion to its ultimate fulfillment. This had been entirely different—a wild mating of two young and healthy animals who behaved completely without restraint.

Her gaze flicked uncertainly to Giles. He smiled gently and raised her fingers to his lips. "Don't look so abashed, Petra. You're probably right about Great-aunt Emmeline. Somewhere she's applauding our initiative."

"I'm not so sure of that," Petra said, but then despite herself she laughed. It had been so utterly glorious that she could regret nothing. Except perhaps that she wasn't sure her legs would hold her up.

"You may have to help me a little," she murmured as they continued their interrupted entry into the house.

"The same here," Giles admitted.

Arms around each other, laughing unreservedly, they made their way into the old house where the very air seemed to stir around them with stern but tolerant acceptance.

The thought of returning to work held no appeal, at least not then. Instead, they found a chilled bottle of champagne and took it and two crystal goblets upstairs to the bathroom. There they soaked in the tub, drinking the champagne and soaping each other until they could most truly be said to be squeaky clean.

Afterward, in the big welcoming bed, they made love again, more gently and slowly but no less fulfilling.

It was, Petra thought, the culmination to a perfect day. Grillas was no longer a problem; she and Giles could concentrate on sorting out their disparate lifestyles; she could have her work, her independence and this magnificent man all at the same time. Everything was possible, nothing was out of reach. Life had never been better.

She fell asleep smiling, blissfully unaware of the man holding her, his gaze watchful and his face set in hard, determined lines.

## Chapter 16

It stormed that night. A low pressure area moving up from the southern Atlantic collided with a Canadian high. The resulting turbulence spawned slashing rains and gale-force winds.

Snug in bed, curled up beside Giles, Petra paid little heed to what was going on outside. The old house had weathered many storms, including ones far worse than this; it barely creaked. A few branches slapped against the windows; some even fell to the ground. But overall, Great-aunt Emmeline's folly rode through the night with the same gracious insouciance it had shown for more than a hundred years.

Not every place was so fortunate. Along the shore, high waves crashed over the breakwaters, sending boats surging at their anchors. Out in the Great Salt

Pond, several of the anchorages failed to hold. A cabin cruiser owned by a real estate developer from New Jersey who had been warned that he was anchoring too far out but had chosen not to pay attention, broke loose of its mooring and went lurching and careering across the pond.

It slammed first into a thirty-seven-foot powerboat named *Zesty Lady*, inflicting extensive damage to the bow section. As the lady began taking on water, the cruiser continued to plow its way inland following the direction of both tide and wind.

Next in its path was a twenty-foot catamaran that managed through sheer serendipity to swerve out of the way at the last possible moment, thereby avoiding the loss of a significant portion of one of its hulls.

Dead ahead lay *Feng-p'o-p'o*, properly anchored at what should have been a safe distance from both the shore and any other vessel. Should have been, but wasn't.

For a few moments the wind died away and the cruiser rocked on the waves, awkward and uncertain as an inebriated guest who continues to gyrate on the dance floor after the music has stopped. But then another gust tore through the inlet and across the pond, picking up the cruiser, restoring its mad energy, and sending it smashing into the magnificent schooner.

The harsh splintering of wood rang above the wind. *Feng-p'o-p'o* rocked backward on her keel for long perilous seconds before the superb symmetry of her design automatically righted her. She swayed on the water, proud and defiant, but a wounded goddess trailing her shattered jib.

The cruiser continued on its way. It struck two more smaller boats and sideswept a third before running aground at last on a stretch of beach adjacent to a house occupied by the remnants of a 1960s commune. Its members had settled on the island shortly after the first military advisers were sent to Vietnam. There they had remained through war, social upheaval and technological revolution.

When the cabin cruiser came to a halt with its prow sticking through the railing of their porch, the two male and three female members of the Aquarius Ascending family emerged dazedly to inspect it. Having hoisted themselves on board, a bit gingerly since they weren't kids anymore, they discovered half-a-dozen miraculously unbroken bottles of cognac, a freezer full of strip steaks, enough video equipment to stock a small store and an extensive lady's and gentleman's wardrobe that ran heavily to spandex and gold chains. They spent the night stripping the boat, consuming the cognac and steaks while hiding the rest in the root cellar under the house.

By the following morning, as the frantic owner of the cabin cruiser was attempting to raise his insurance carrier, the harbor master was on the phone to the owners of the damaged boats.

Giles put the receiver down with an angry click. He had been awakened from the light sleep he'd fallen into around dawn. His head hurt, his nerves were strained, and he just plain didn't need this.

"We have to get dressed," he said as he got out of bed.

Snug in her nest, Petra blinked at him. "Why?"

"The boat took some damage last night. I need to check her out."

Visions of several hours of uninterrupted work danced in Petra's head. After the day and night just concluded, she felt energized, invigorated and ready to ace the rest of the book. If she could only get some time alone.

"Go ahead," she said. "I'll be fine here."

Giles shook his head. "I think you should come with me."

Petra frowned. This was getting out of hand. She sat up in the bed and looked at him directly. "I really need to work, and besides, I'll just be in the way. You go."

Still he hesitated. Realistically he knew she was right—they both needed some time on their own. But his gut instinct, the same one that had kept him alive in China, said not to let her out of his sight.

Against his better judgment, driven by the stark need to make her happy, he said, "All right."

Petra didn't quite breathe a sigh of relief, but she looked like she was close to it. When he left a few minutes later, she sent him on his way with a cheerful smile and a wave.

Alone, she stretched luxuriously under the covers but wasted no time relaxing. Instead, she dressed quickly, went downstairs to the kitchen and fixed herself some coffee. With that in hand, she padded into the small parlor she was using to work.

Before the coffee had cooled enough to drink, she was caught up in the photos. They involved her completely as she rapidly and efficiently made the selections for the final chapters. As always, captions would be kept to a minimum, merely identifying the place and date when the photo was taken. Petra made it a policy never to identify any of her subjects by name, although the more publicity-conscious members of the Manhattan social circus had offered her inordinate amounts of money to do so. She never failed to be astounded and amused by the lengths people would go to in order to be associated with photographs that were too starkly honest ever to be flattering.

About an hour into the work, she paused for a moment to freshen her cup of coffee. She was coming back from the kitchen when the doorbell rang.

Daryl was peering through the etched glass panel. He smiled when he saw her and waved. "Hi," he said when she opened the door.

"Hi," Petra repeated hesitantly. Daryl's natural habitat was Manhattan and the Hamptons. Seeing him anywhere else was like seeing a tree growing upside down in space, its roots wafting gently in the breeze.

"What are you doing here?" she asked, making no bones about it. If he was going to act so blatantly out of character, he had to expect questions like that.

"Let me come in," he said cheerfully, "and I'll tell you all about it."

She felt a tiny surge of uncertainty, knowing that Giles wouldn't approve. It was his house, after all. But then it would also be awfully rude to turn Daryl away.

"All right," she said as she stood aside to admit him. Just to make sure he understood where they both stood, she added, "Giles should be back soon."

Daryl stood in the entry hall, hands thrust into the pockets of his meticulously tailored cords and gazed around him. "Ah, yes, the enterprising Professor Chastain. I never did get to say ta-ta to him the other night." He turned and eyed her directly. "Or you, either, as I recall. Are you terribly involved with him?"

The abruptness of the question—and its unswerving directness—threw Petra, but she recovered quickly. "Yes, I am."

His face stiffened, but he transformed himself almost instantly, even managing a stilted laugh. "How nice, love in bloom and all that. How about some coffee?"

He followed her into the kitchen and flopped down at the big oak table. She set a mug in front of him and took a chair opposite.

"Now tell me, what brings you here?"

"Fate," Daryl said with a lopsided grin. "I was sailing off West Hampton—" Petra nodded at this confirmation of her thoughts "—when that storm kicked up. I had my work cut out for me staying afloat last night. This morning I decided to make for the nearest safe harbor, which turned out to be here. Daphne had mentioned that you were visiting, so I made a few inquiries and tracked you down."

"You must be exhausted," Petra said, her sympathy aroused by the implication of a night spent battling the wind and sea. As much as she loved sailing, she didn't envy Daryl. "Would you like something to eat?"

He shook his head. "Thanks, but I don't think my tum-tum's up to it. The coffee's good though...and just seeing you—" He was silent for a moment, sitting with his head bent and his hands around the cup. Finally he said, "So you and the Professor are really hitting it off?"

Petra flushed slightly. Her relationship with Giles was still so new and unsettling that there were flashes of time when she had trouble believing it was real. Talking about it with another person was difficult.

"I know we don't seem to have that much in common on the surface, but we get along very well." Especially now that Giles seemed willing to recognize her need for a little solitude from time to time.

"I wouldn't say that about you," Daryl murmured. "You and Chastain actually seem to be a lot alike."

Surprised, Petra asked, "What do you mean?"

"You're both loners...you go your own way, make your own rules, and everything you want just seems to work out for you." Before Petra could even attempt to refute this, he went on, "Did you know Chastain was in China? He stayed on even after the government killed all those kids. The word is he was doing some kind of undercover work for Washington. The Chinese were about to arrest him when he finally got out. Most men wouldn't have squeaked through, but he did. Came home covered with glory, landed a plum job at one of the top universities and then chucked it when he decided Washington wasn't for him.''

Petra took a long sip of her coffee and studied Daryl. He looked very pale and his hands shook. Quietly she asked, ''How do you know all this?''

''I asked around. No harm in that, is there? Anyway, he's still in very tight with our government, has contacts all over the place. He can write his own ticket any time he wants.''

''I don't think he's really interested in going back to Washington,'' Petra said. At least, she hoped he wasn't. From the little he'd said about Amanda, she'd gotten the impression he was really over that. But sweet Lord, what if he wasn't?

She was too bogged down thinking about that to notice the tight, ugly look that distorted Daryl's picture-book features. Harshly he said, ''You're not getting the point, dearest. On your own, you were bad enough, clicking away with those god-awful cameras, snapping people when they least expected it. But I could deal with that. Hooking up with Chastain changed the equation.''

He reached across the table, his hand closing around her wrist. ''Changed it drastically. You showed him the pictures, didn't you?''

''P-pictures...?'' This couldn't be happening. What was Daryl talking about and what had happened to the charming, rather vacuous man he'd always been? In his place was a cold, remote stranger who was staring at her with overly bright eyes and a twisted smile.

"The pictures for that stupid book of yours. I need them and I am going to get them. And after all the trouble you've put me to, I'm not going to be very nice about it."

Petra swallowed. Her heart was beating painfully hard. She was dazed by her own obtuseness, her own failure to see what should have been smack in front of her face.

Grillas hadn't been alone in that photo. He'd been with Daryl, talking to him in a way that suggested they were, at the very least, familiar with each other.

"You're too late," she said as firmly as she could manage.

Daryl's face paled further. He tightened his hand on her wrist until she winced in pain. "What do you mean?"

"The DEA already knows about Grillas being in New York and attending that party. Furthermore, Grillas knows he was photographed and that the DEA's seen the evidence of his presence."

"You're lying!"

"I'm not! Grillas doesn't care. He thinks it's funny."

Daryl emitted a low, virulent curse. He let go of her abruptly and stood up, but when Petra also tried to rise, he thrust her back into the seat.

"You damned bitch!"

The sheer rage in his face froze her. She stared unmoving as he snarled, "I had to keep it from Grillas. I *had* to. He's totally intolerant of any kind of failure. So he thinks it's funny, does he? He also thinks it's funny to kill people—very slowly. And that's exactly what he's going to do unless I can convince him I've made up for my slip-up."

"I don't understand," Petra said desperately. "Why are you involved with Grillas, and how can his being photographed be blamed on you?"

"You don't know anything, do you?" Daryl sneered. He dragged her upright and slammed her against the kitchen wall, his face so close to hers that he blocked out the rest of the room. "You're supposed to be some brilliant chronicler of your times, but you don't see anything beyond the tip of your own nose."

"I see plenty," Petra shot back, refusing to be cowed by him no matter how great her growing terror. She had miscalculated badly; the only question was how much she would have to pay for it. With reckless courage, she went on, "I see a man who had everything handed to him on a silver platter but who for some reason didn't find it enough, so he hooked up with a cold-blooded mass murderer. That's what drug dealers are—killers not just of individuals but of families, communities, maybe even our whole society if they aren't stopped soon."

Overwhelmed by her anger, she looked at him in disgust. "You had millions of dollars, respect, position, security. Why wasn't it enough? Why did you have to involve yourself with Grillas?"

A pulse pounded in Daryl's forehead. His eyes were reddened, his mouth pulled to a thin, white line. "Because I'm an addict, you stupid bitch! Do you think

I'd go near him if I weren't? But I have to have what he sells, and he . . . he found out about me." His voice broke. For a moment, the enraged strength seemed to ebb from him. But he recovered at least partly. His voice was lower and more controlled as he said, "He bled me dry. Oh, not directly. He used intermediaries, people who pretended to be my friends, who were always happy to see me and tell me how great I was. And I really was, at least for a while. It seemed like I couldn't do anything wrong. Everything I touched turned to gold. But then the damn stock market crashed and everything went sour. No matter which way I turned, I lost money. And not just a little. I *hemorrhaged* money, and I still needed drugs. I needed them more than ever. So Grillas made me an offer. He set me up in business, covered my losses, let me go on being what I'd always been. All I had to do was launder cash for him."

He laughed weakly at the memory. "It was easy. I just kept on making deals as though I were using my own money. But I didn't have any of my own left. It was all his, only he let me pretend . . . let me go on believing that I was still me . . . still alive . . . still real."

He took a long, deep breath and caught her face between his hands, compelling her to meet his eyes. "Don't you understand? I can't risk having him turn on me. Without him, I won't be anything."

"It's too late," Petra said through taut lips. "He knows."

*"Nooo!"*

She screamed as Daryl threw her from him. Petra's head struck the edge of the stove. Pain shot through her. Desperately she struggled against it only to find that she could not. Whirling darkness drew her into unconsciousness.

## Chapter 17

A sharp persistent pain between her shoulders nudged Petra back into the world. She lifted her head slowly, unaware for a moment of where she was or what had happened.

Memory flooded back with terrifying swiftness. She tried to move, only to discover that she couldn't. Strong ropes secured her to a kitchen chair.

Through the open door, she could see Daryl across the hall in the room where she had been working. Photos were scattered over the floor, files were upturned, all the careful order she had worked to achieve was undone.

Under the circumstances that didn't matter much. She had far more immediate concerns.

As though sensing her return to consciousness, he looked up. Their eyes met.

"Where is it?" he shouted.

Petra refused to answer. She was afraid that if she told him the truth—that the photo had been sent to her loft in New York—he would become even more enraged. At any rate, the negative was still in the box he had overturned, but it comprised a single frame among hundreds of strips of film. His chances of finding it were negligible.

Unfortunately Daryl came to the same conclusion.

He stood up, dusting off the knees of his perfectly tailored trousers. Even now, looking at him, Petra had difficulty believing what was happening. He was so boyishly handsome, so appealingly put together, so seemingly harmless. The contrast between the way he appeared and the way he was, left her with an overwhelming sense of unreality.

The thrust of her work had always been that people's outward appearance when dispassionately observed revealed inner truths about them. She still believed that, but now she had to face the fact that there were exceptions, people whose inner landscape bore no relation to the face they presented to the world.

Daryl smiled down at her. He stood directly in front of her, showing no sign of the anger he had exhibited moments before. Instead, he seemed relaxed and in good humor.

"You know," he said pleasantly, "sometimes I'm so smart it surprises me."

Wrenching fear coiled through Petra. No matter how she turned that around, it didn't sound good.

"What do you mean?"

"There's an obvious solution to this problem. I can't find the photo, there are simply too many to look through." His smile turned gently chiding. "And you're not being very cooperative, sweetheart. So the obvious solution is to just get rid of everything."

He glanced around, nodding. "This is a really old house, isn't it? I shouldn't have any problem at all." Abruptly he turned and headed for the kitchen door. "I'll be back in a jiff." He laughed as he added, "Don't go anywhere."

Barely had the door closed behind him than Petra began frantic efforts to do exactly that. She pulled with all her strength on the ropes holding her arms, but nothing she did budged them. The same was true with those securing her ankles to the bottom rung of the chair. No matter how she tried, she achieved nothing but bruised and abraded limbs.

Tears stung her eyes, not so much from the pain as from fear and frustration. She blinked them back quickly as Daryl returned. Under no circumstances would she allow him to see the effect this was having on her.

"Found it," he said triumphantly.

Petra froze. He was holding a handful of oil-soaked rags.

"I was hoping for gasoline," he admitted, "but the can's empty. Anyway, these ought to do the job without any difficulty."

"Daryl," Petra said hoarsely, "what are you doing?"

He looked at her in surprise. "I told you, taking care of the problem. You should pay more attention."

"Y-you're going to burn the photos?"

"Of course, it's the obvious solution." He frowned slightly, as though not sure he was getting his point across. "You do see that, don't you?"

Petra's throat was so dry that she could barely speak. "Uh...sure...I guess. You're going to take the photos outside and burn them?"

"No, of course not. I'm going to burn them right here. This old house should go up without any trouble at all." He smiled again as though excusing her slowness. "I'm going to burn everything, sweetheart. There's really nothing else I can do."

Petra swallowed hard against the bile burning the back of her throat and struggled to remain calm. Panic would avail her nothing. She was dealing with a madman and nothing would save her except her own wits.

"Daryl...you don't really want to hurt anyone."

He looked taken aback at the mere notion. "Of course I don't. But as I just said, I don't have any choice. I'm doing this because of you, Petra. You forced me into it." He paused for a moment, considering. "I only hope it's not too traumatic. I want to put this behind me as quickly as possible."

Petra's control broke. Terror-stricken and furiously angry at the same time, she cried, *"You're talking about murder."*

He shrugged. "You could call it that, I suppose. To me it's merely self-preservation. Besides, no one will ever know."

"Of course they will! It'll be obvious that this is arson."

"I realize there's a possibility of that," Daryl said with exaggerated patience. "But the authorities will think one of Grillas's people did it. Since my involvement with him isn't known, no one will suspect me." He smiled contentedly. "I'll be free and clear."

Petra stared at him in horror. He was absolutely right. That the arson would be discovered didn't matter, unless Daryl could be linked to it.

"Giles will suspect you," she said desperately. "He'll tell the authorities and they'll start asking questions. Someone must have seen you come ashore this morning. You'll be recognized."

He laughed patronizingly. "I came ashore yesterday afternoon and holed up in an empty house. This morning before anyone else was out and about, I came here. I was watching from behind the hedges when Chastain left. No one's seen me and no one's going to. I'll wait until after dark to leave."

He lifted the rags in mock salute. "Nice try, sweetheart, but it's not going to work."

He went across the hall to the small parlor. She could hear him moving around, gathering the photos up and laying the rags wherever he thought they would be most effective. The stench of oil lingered in the kitchen, making her want to gag.

"That should do it," Daryl murmured as he returned. He bent over to check the ropes securing her. Petra flinched at his touch, but he seemed not to notice. Absently he said, "I wish I had a few more rags for in here, but the fire should spread quickly enough."

He straightened up and gave her a quick smile. "Don't worry, I understand the smoke kills people before the fire ever reaches them."

She shook her head frantically. Her courage was gone and her pride with it. "Please," she said faintly, "don't do this, Daryl. You need help and you can get it. You can be free of Grillas. Just don't do this."

He looked down at her, puzzled. "Why would I want to be free of Grillas? As long as I stay out of trouble with him, I've got money, power and drugs. What could be better?"

Petra had no answer for that. With the death of her hopes, all the strength seemed to go out of her. She could only stare in mute horror as Daryl took a box of kitchen matches from the stove and with a final nod to her, vanished into the parlor.

An instant later, she heard the rasp of the match head against the box and the quick hiss of flame that followed.

"Thanks," Giles said as he stepped off the dinghy onto the beach. He nodded cordially to the man who had ferried him over to *Feng-p'o-p'o.*

The harbormaster nodded. He was an older man, white-haired with a weathered face and a no-nonsense manner. In his ten years of trying to protect the island's fragile waterways, he'd seen a great deal. Nothing much surprised him, but he was still exasperated by the foolishness people could get up to when they wanted.

"That's a beautiful boat you've got," he said to Giles. "Good thing she can be repaired. That fellow from Jersey, the one whose cruiser got loose, claims he's fully insured."

"I hope so for his sake," Giles said. He was in no mood for tolerance. The damage to the schooner wasn't as severe as it might have been. There were craftspeople on the island who could replace her jib without difficulty. But had the cruiser struck a few meters closer in, the outcome would have been very different. Then her entire hull would have been threatened and she might well have sunk.

"If it's any consolation to you," the harbormaster said, "when we found his boat this morning, there wasn't much left. Those Aquarius folks took everything including the plumbing. 'Course, they're not admitting that, and by the time we get a warrant to search their place, they'll have moved everything out, anyway."

"I can't say I'm sorry," Giles said. "Maybe he'll take the hint and stay off the water from now on."

The harbormaster shrugged. Only time would tell, but in the meanwhile, he was grateful there had been only property damage and no loss of life.

"I'll give you a call when we get straight on the insurance," he said.

Giles climbed the beach to the road where he'd left the Land Rover. As he got behind the wheel, he debated what to do. He needed to check in with the boat yard and make arrangements for the repair. As long as he was out, he should also stop at the bank and the post office. By the time he got all that done, he hoped Petra would have had enough of her own company. Whether she had or not, he didn't intend leaving her alone again, at least not until the situation with Grillas was cleared up to his own satisfaction.

He felt a small twinge of regret about not being completely frank with her. Maybe he should have told her about his suspicions concerning Daryl. Unburdened by any friendship with the man, he'd seen the potential significance of the photograph when Petra did not. He could have said something, but he was used to making whatever decisions were needed without consulting anyone else.

As he started the engine, he smiled faintly. Petra would be mad at him if she ever found out, but he could handle that. The pleasure of their making up almost made it worth getting her riled.

His smile deepened as he contemplated the hot, sweet passion they had shared the previous day. For a woman who had been a virgin not very long ago, she was learning at a remarkable clip. A man would have his work cut out keeping up with her. But that was all right; there was never anything he liked better than a challenge.

He turned the vehicle onto the beach road and headed for the boat yard, resolved to handle the business there as quickly as possible. The rest of the chores could wait. Just thinking about Petra made him ache for her.

Petra was also aching, but for far less pleasant reasons. Her throat throbbed from the screams that had been a desperate but unsuccessful effort to get help. Smoke burned her eyes and made her cough painfully. Her arms and legs throbbed from her continued struggle with the unyielding ropes.

Through the door leading from the kitchen, she could watch the steady, insidious spread of the fire. It moved like a living creature beyond the immediate circle defined by the heap of photographs. Already one side of the couch had begun to smolder and the small table beside it was catching quickly.

Beyond the couch lay a brace of tall windows bracketed by heavy velvet curtains. Once the fire reached them, the entire wall would be engulfed almost at once. And then . . .

Desperately Petra turned her head away. There was nothing to be gained from watching the progress of the fire. She had to concentrate all her energies on freeing herself.

Except that there didn't seem to be any way of doing that. By jerking herself from one side to the other, she was able to maneuver the chair a few feet. But the door to the outside lay several yards away and the room was filling rapidly with smoke.

A sob broke from her. She wanted desperately to live not only for her own sake but also for Giles. They had found something rare and precious together. So what if it wasn't absolutely perfect and problem-free? They could work things out if only they had the chance.

But that chance was vanishing rapidly in the swirling clouds of smoke and the crackling rush of flame. Eventually the fire would be seen and help summoned. But the windows were still closed against the morning chill. Long, vital minutes would pass before enough smoke reached the outside to attract any notice.

And still the door remained torturously out of reach.

In all her life, Petra had never felt so desperately alone and afraid. Not even when she was a small child torn between callous and selfish parents had she known such a sense of overriding hopelessness. She teetered on the edge of despair, but before she could fall over into it, something cracked open within her. From some deep, hidden reserve came the will to go on fighting so long as a last breath remained.

Slowly, methodically, using every ounce of her strength and courage, she maneuvered the chair across the kitchen floor until she finally reached the door. Only to realize what in her desperation she had not allowed herself to contemplate. The door was closed. With her hands bound behind her, she had no way of opening it.

Still, she refused to give up. The image of Giles in all the ways she had seen him—lover, friend, companion, sometimes even adversary—drew her on. She could not—she would not—surrender to death when life promised such sweetness.

Ahead of her to the left and almost directly at her eye level was the switch controlling the kitchen lights. Beside it was a second switch, newly installed to control the floodlights on the roof.

At night, the lights were clearly visible. During the day they were far less so. It was barely a glimmer of a chance, but it was the only one Petra had.

She bent her head, pushing the switch first up, then down...up and down...on and off...blinking the lights and praying all the while that someone, somehow, would see her desperate signal.

Giles paused at a stop sign, waiting as two mopeds and a cluster of pedestrians passed before he began to make the left turn that would take him into town. Further ahead, about a quarter-mile down the road was his house, its gabled roof peeking above the trees.

Absently he glanced in its direction.

The floodlights were on.

Giles frowned. He could have sworn he'd flipped the lights off as he left the house that morning. He squinted and looked again.

He must have been mistaken a moment before; the lights were off.

A horn blared behind him. He shook his head and began the left turn, only to glance toward the house again.

The lights were on.

*What the hell...?*

The horn sounded again, but this time Giles ignored it, as he ignored the startled looks of the pedestrians who jumped back onto the side of the road just in time to avoid the Land Rover as it roared past.

Even allowing for the long, twisting dirt road leading to it, Giles reached the house in under three minutes by the simple expedient of shoving the gas pedal down as far as it would go and keeping it there.

Barely had he screeched to a halt than he was out of the car and running toward the house.

*"Petra,"* he called as he thrust open the front door. He smelled the smoke instantly. Terror flowed through him, blocking out every other sensation.

*"Petra!"*

"Giles, go back! There's a fire! Go around the other way."

And waste precious seconds in the process. He never even considered it.

Flames were licking at the mahogany paneling in the hallway. Heat reached out to scorch his face and arms. Smoke filled his eyes and lungs. But Giles was conscious of none of that. He had no thought except to reach Petra. Nothing else, not even his own life, mattered.

When he found her, huddled against the kitchen door, relief poured through him. Until he saw the ropes holding her to the chair and realized fully what must have happened.

Petra took one look into his eyes and averted her own. She had never seen such absolute, deadly rage in a man. Beside Giles, Daryl's anger was like the puny thrashings of a small boy. She had no idea of what to say or do, but neither was necessary.

Giles made no attempt to free her from the chair. He merely lifted her right along with it, kicked open the kitchen door that had thwarted her and carried her straight outside. He deposited her a safe distance from the house, but then, incredibly, turned back toward it.

"What are you doing?" she screamed. "Don't go in there again."

"All your work," he said. "Your photos. They're still in there."

"They're gone! But it wouldn't matter if they weren't. For God's sake, you're what counts!"

He went very still, staring at her for a long moment. But when he spoke, his voice was rigidly controlled. "Where's Daryl?"

Petra stared at him in bewilderment. "How did you know?"

A look of painful self-recrimination passed over Giles's hard features. "I didn't, I suspected. But I should have said something to you all the same. That's for later. Right now, where is he?"

"I don't know, he left right after he started the fire. Look, just get me out of these."

At that moment, she wanted more than anything to be free of the ropes. Free to go to the man she loved, to embrace and reassure him. Free to get help for the magnificent old house. Free to do so many things she had thought might be lost to her forever.

But she hadn't quite counted on how Giles would free her.

Cold steel flashed in the sunlight. Petra bit back a scream as the ropes holding her snapped like so much taffy.

"Do you always carry that thing?" she asked as she rubbed her lacerated wrists.

"I thought I might need it on the boat," he replied shortly. "Did he say anything that might indicate where he went?"

Petra looked past him to the house. Smoke was pouring from the windows. So far, only the back section seemed involved, but soon enough the entire structure would be engulfed.

"Forget Daryl," she pleaded. "We have to get help."

"What did he say?" Giles demanded. He didn't so much as glance toward the house. For him it might not have existed. All his attention was focused on the man who had harmed Petra, who had almost taken her life, and who would be made to pay for that no matter what the cost.

"He said he would hide out until after dark...to avoid being seen. We've got to call the fire department, the police. Come on!"

Frantically she tugged at his arm. He remained unmoving. "What else?"

"You're crazy! You'll never find him. He hid out last night somewhere on the island in an empty house. He was watching this morning when you left. He's crazy, but he's also clever. Just let him go, can't you?"

"An empty house...but close enough for him to be watching this place in the morning?" Abruptly Giles nodded. "All right. Take the Land Rover and go for help. Tell whoever you find I'm heading for the Hamden place."

"H-Hamden..."

"On the bluffs east of here. It's the closest house to here, and it's empty. My guess is that's where he is."

"No," Petra protested. "You can't face him alone. He's nuts, there's no telling what he might do."

Giles smiled coldly. "But I know exactly what I'm going to do. Now go." He pushed her gently toward the vehicle.

Petra went, only because she realized that any further effort to argue with him would be futile. They were wasting time. She had to get help for the house, but more importantly she had to get help to stop Giles. She couldn't let him risk his life against Daryl.

Damned infuriating, stubborn man.

No wonder she loved him so much.

# Chapter 18

In the summer of his eighth year, Giles had been taken on a hunting trip by several of his uncles. The intention had been good, to help a fatherless boy forge bonds to other men who would be his role models. But the outcome had been far less positive.

Giles still remembered his excitement at being included in the trip, the thrill of acceptance and the half-guilty, heady delight of entering an exclusively male domain. He'd soaked up the lore of tracking and hunting as though it was the wisdom of the ages. No detail, no nuance had escaped his rapt attention.

He shared fully in the surge of strength and excitement that came when the quarry was sighted. The stag was magnificent, carrying a full head of antlers, weighing in easily at several hundred pounds. He

crashed through the underbrush at full speed, pressing the hunters to their limit, until one got off a shot
that took him down.

Only then, in the sudden silence that followed the
animal's death thrashes, had Giles's bright pleasure in
the experience died, too. He stared down at the blood-
splattered animal, seeing the light fade from his eyes,
and knew a moment of such heart-twisting sorrow that
years later he could still relive it intact.

Barely aware of what he did, he had knelt in the dry
leaves beside the stag. Hot tears trailed down his
smooth child's cheeks. He felt no shame that he cried;
indeed, at that moment it seemed the only reasonable
thing to do. The tears that had remained sealed within
him when he was orphaned were released at last for the
mighty but ultimately helpless creature before him.

Later, several of the men looked at him askance and
murmured among themselves that poor old Chastain's kid was turning out to be a wimp. Giles had
heard them, but their words had not touched the cen-
tral core of his being. Even then he had understood
instinctively that their condemnation was wrong.

So had his youngest uncle, who had taken him aside
and talked to him gently about what had happened. "I
guess we shouldn't have brought you," he said.
"You've been through an awful lot lately and this was
just too much. But—" Here he hesitated, unsure of
how much to say to an eight-year-old boy. But a boy
who looked at him with such steady self-containment
that honesty had seemed the only possible response.

"Sometimes," his uncle said, "life gets very rough. Sometimes we have to do things that frighten and horrify us. Sometimes we even have to kill." He shrugged apologetically. "It's easier if you've done it before, that's all. It makes it a little less tough to live with."

Giles supposed his uncle had been right, although he had never hunted again. He understood that for certain men the ritual of killing was both a release from the tensions of their lives and a preparation for the even rougher times. For him, it wasn't. For him, anger burned out all else and prepared him as nothing else ever could have.

He was going to nail Daryl Ellis. He was going to take the man who had dared to try to kill Petra and make him regret ever having drawn breath.

And he was going to enjoy doing it.

The bluffs lay directly ahead, rising in all their magnificent wildness. Few houses remained on them, some having already been lost to erosion, others abandoned. The Hamden place was a small gray-clapboard bungalow that had seen little repair over the years as its owners realistically prepared for its eventual loss. Four decades before, when it was built, it had stood so far back from the edge of the cliff that it had seemed completely safe. But nature had worked more quickly and forcibly than anyone had expected. Already, part of what had been the front lawn was gone, and a section of fence had been lost.

But a few trees remained, and Giles used them for cover as he approached the house. He moved swiftly and determinedly, his superbly conditioned body responding without effort.

The shades were pulled down in all the windows. One of the screens hung off its frame, and a few twigs were caught in the latticework door. The whole place had an air of emptiness, as though no one had set foot in it for at least several weeks.

The wind that blew incessantly over the island had flattened the scrub grass that grew all around the house. It seemed to be uniformly smooth, but Giles could make out slight footprints that crossed the grass to the front door.

He bent lower, ran swiftly and reached the side of the house without incident.

There he waited, listening intently until he was sure no one was moving around inside. When he was convinced, he stood up, lifted the thick tree branch he had brought with him, and smashed it directly through the kitchen window.

Screen and glass gave way with crashing force. Barely had the shards stopped falling than Giles had vaulted through the window. He sprang upright and looked around hastily.

Footsteps thudded down the small hall, only to pause at the entrance to the kitchen. Hardly breathing, Giles stood poised and ready behind the swinging door. Daryl entered slowly, a small, snub-nosed pistol in his right hand. He glanced toward the shattered window.

"How the hell . . . ?"

The words were barely formed when Giles was on him. Coming from behind, he slammed an arm around Daryl's throat, cutting off his air, and with the other hand grabbed for the gun.

The two men struggled. Daryl was younger, well built and in relatively good shape. Giles was stronger, more finely honed, and fueled by rock-hard determination. Even so, the contest was almost even. Faced with an attack on the only thing he really cared about—himself—Daryl exploded. He fought with the fury of the deranged. For long, desperate minutes, the fight went back and forth, until finally Giles succeeded in wrenching the gun from Daryl's hand. It flew across the room, landing against the far wall.

Giles made a dive to reach it, a calculated risk that fell only inches short of succeeding. The split-second break gave Daryl the chance he needed. He broke from the kitchen and ran out of the bungalow.

Giles followed. The wind had picked up; whirling sand stung their faces. Twenty feet from the edge of the cliff, Giles hurled himself at the other man. He brought him down hard. The two grappled, turning over and over, heading straight toward the edge.

Giles realized it first. Dodging to avoid a gouging blow to his eyes, he tried to pull back. In doing so, he released his hold on Daryl just long enough for the other man to stagger to his feet. Swiftly Giles did the same. The two stood, facing each other, both torn and bloodied, breathing hard.

"You surprise me, professor," Daryl said between harsh gasps of breath. He smiled mockingly. "I didn't think you had it in you."

Giles stared at him. A mad light burned in the younger man's eyes. He looked infinitely dangerous and completely confident. Behind him, inches from where he stood, the cliff fell away to glistening boulders and white-foamed waves.

"It won't do you any good," Daryl said. "You can't beat me, nobody can. I'm invincible."

"You're insane," Giles said softly. The words were meant for himself at least as much as for Daryl. In all the cold, ruthless rush to catch this man, he had not considered what he would find when he did. Now he saw.

Looking back at him, staring him straight in the face, he saw the final product of violence in its most insidious form. The violence Daryl had perpetrated against himself to destroy his own humanity.

Slowly he took a step back, his hands at his sides.

"All right, I'm not going to try to stop you. Come away from the cliff."

Daryl laughed. He bounced up and down on the balls of his feet. Sand and a few tufts of grass crumbled beneath him. "It's too late to give up. You know about me, I have to kill you. The same way I have to kill her."

"You don't have to do anything. Just move away. You're right on the edge...."

Off in the distance, Giles caught the sound of sirens coming fast. He redoubled his efforts.

"Come on, there's no reason to stay there. I'm not going to try anything."

The sirens grew louder. Daryl heard them, too. His smile vanished. "They're coming."

"It doesn't matter. You'll be okay. Come on." Giles held out his hand.

Daryl stared at it. When he looked back up, his eyes were fathomless pools reflecting nothing. He tossed his head, the breeze lifting his hair. For a moment, he looked completely restored—young, handsome, whole.

He smiled again.

"Did you know," he said, "that I can fly?"

The police had gone as had the firemen. The smell of smoke still filled the house. Part of the exterior wall on the north side was charred where the parlor curtains had caught. The parlor itself was virtually destroyed. The hallway had taken some damage and the kitchen as well, but apart from that the rest of Great-aunt Emmeline's folly was remarkably intact.

"I'm impressed," Petra said drowsily. "The firemen did a great job."

Giles nodded. They were sitting in the Land Rover, taking a last look at the house before leaving it for a few hours. Cleanup could wait until the next day. There would be carpenters to call, electricians, painters, paperhangers... But eventually the damage would be repaired and the house restored. First, though, they both needed a hot meal and a long rest.

"So did the police," he said quietly.

Petra reached out a hand and covered his. "You couldn't have stopped him, Giles. I know, I was there. When he jumped, there was nothing anyone could do."

Daryl's body had been recovered from the rocks below the cliff. A team of rescue workers had brought the blanket-draped stretcher up the steep incline. An ambulance had been standing by, but there was nothing anyone could have done. Daryl had died instantly.

"I wanted to kill him," Giles said starkly. He stared off into space. "When I went after him, that's what I intended."

Petra took a deep breath and let it out slowly. She'd suspected as much. The thought horrified her, but far more important was the fact that in the end, Giles had tried to save Daryl, not destroy him.

She said as much. "You can't blame youself for what you felt. What counts is what you did."

"Maybe," he conceded. He turned and looked at her gently. "I should have told you what I suspected about him instead of keeping it to myself."

She met his eyes calmly. "I should have trusted you more instead of worrying that you were trying to overwhelm and dominate me."

He smiled wryly. "Is that what you thought?"

"It did occur to me," she admitted.

"You weren't completely wrong. I've been afraid of losing you from the beginning. I think I probably held on too tightly to compensate for that."

"Afraid . . . ?" Petra repeated slowly. "It's hard to think of you that way. You always seem so . . . indomitable."

"I'm not," he said somberly. "I'm just a man with all the usual fears and weaknesses. I fell in love with a woman who seemed to look at life a lot differently than I and who values her independence above all else."

"Valued," Petra said softly.

"What?"

"I did value my independence above all else when I was afraid of getting too close to anyone." She smiled gently. "Or maybe I just hadn't met the right person. But I have now. I love you, Giles Chastain, and there's nothing I want more than to be with you."

A Land Rover is a difficult place to kiss, but they managed it. Only the gearshift sticking into them finally forced them apart. Laughing and breathless, they gazed at each other.

"I can sell the loft . . ." Petra began.

"I can sell the house . . ." Giles said.

They stopped, shook their heads and started over.

"Don't you dare think of selling Great-aunt Emmeline's house," Petra said. "It happens to be your dowry, and if you think I'm taking you without it, you're nuts."

"Some dowry," Giles said with a grin. "How's a city girl going to work this far from civilization? Besides," he added more seriously, "almost all the photographs and negatives for your new book were destroyed. You'll need to be in New York to take them again.''

She shook her head. ''I can't start that project over, Giles. It's finished for me and maybe it's best this way. For all the glitz and glitter, Daryl's world was a grim place. Besides, I've got better things to do.'' She looked out over the water to a horizon where a few scattered lights were beginning to shine.

''I want to take more pictures of people like Dave and his family, people who are struggling to maintain a way of life they care about deeply. And I want to take pictures of this island, to show both its beauty and its fragility. People need to know more about how rare and precious places like this really are so that they'll help take better care of them.''

''Great,'' Giles said slowly. He reached out a hand to touch her cheek with infinite gentleness. ''But aren't there any pictures you still want to take in New York?''

She frowned slightly. ''Why do you ask?''

''Because as much as I like living here and being a writer, I really miss teaching.'' He shrugged, looking faintly embarrassed. ''Columbia's made me an offer I'd have to be nuts to turn down. They want me to start with the fall term.''

''That's in just a couple of weeks.''

''I know,'' he said, ignoring the gearshift to reach for her again. ''But if we hurry, we can still squeeze in a honeymoon.''

"Marriage," Petra said awhile later when the gear-shift had won another round. "Honeymoons, keeping house, children."

"Children," Giles echoed just a bit faintly.

"Children," Petra said firmly. "Next thing, I'll be baking bread."

Giles grimaced. "You have many wonderful qualities, darling, but I'll bake the bread. After all," he added as he switched the engine on and turned the Land Rover toward the long, winding road, "this is going to be a thoroughly modern marriage."

"Hmmm," Petra said. She snuggled back against the seat and looked at him from the corner of her eye. "I don't know about that." Slowly a smile lit her face, banishing all the doubts and fears of the past. "But I do know it's going to be a fascinating one."

\* \* \* \* \*

*Silhouette Intimate Moments®*

## Intimate Moments brings you two gripping stories by Emilie Richards

*June*

# Runaway
### by EMILIE RICHARDS
**Intimate Moments #337**

*July*

# The Way Back Home
### by EMILIE RICHARDS
**Intimate Moments #341**

Krista and Rosie Jensen were two sisters who had it all—until a painful secret tore them apart.

They were two special women who met two very special men who made life a little easier—and love a whole lot better—until the day when Krista and Rosie could be sisters once again.

Look for THE WAY BACK HOME, the sequel to RUNAWAY, available now at your favorite retail outlet. If you missed RUNAWAY, or wish to order THE WAY BACK HOME, send your name, address, zip or postal code along with a check or money order for $2.95 for each book ordered, plus 75¢ postage and handling, payable to Silhouette Reader Service to:

In the U.S.
901 Fuhrmann Blvd.
Box 1396
Buffalo, NY 14269-1396

In Canada
P.O. Box 609
Fort Erie, Ontario
L2A 5X3

Please specify book title with your order.

*Silhouette Books®*

RUN-1AA

**Diana Palmer's fortieth story for Silhouette ... chosen
as an Award of Excellence title!**

# CONNAL
# Diana Palmer

Next month, Diana Palmer's bestselling LONG, TALL
TEXANS series continues with CONNAL. The skies
get cloudy on C. C. Tremayne's home on the range
when Penelope Mathews decides to protect him—by
marrying him!

One specially selected title receives the Award of
Excellence every month. Look for CONNAL in August
at your favorite retail outlet ... only from Silhouette
Romance.

## SILHOUETTE'S "BIG WIN"
## SWEEPSTAKES RULES & REGULATIONS
### NO PURCHASE NECESSARY TO ENTER OR RECEIVE A PRIZE

**Back by popular demand, some of Diana Palmer's earliest published books are available again!**

Several years ago, Diana Palmer began her writing career. Sweet, compelling and totally unforgettable, these are the love stories that enchanted readers everywhere.

Next month, six more of these wonderful stories will be available in DIANA PALMER DUETS—Books 4, 5 and 6. Each DUET contains two powerful stories plus an introduction by Diana Palmer. Don't miss:

| | |
|---|---|
| Book Four | **AFTER THE MUSIC**<br>**DREAM'S END** |
| Book Five | **BOUND BY A PROMISE**<br>**PASSION FLOWER** |
| Book Six | **TO HAVE AND TO HOLD**<br>**THE COWBOY AND THE LADY** |